# LOVE
## AND
# MUDDY
# PUDDLES

*A Coco and Charlie Franks novel*

Cecily Anne Paterson

Published by Cecily Anne Paterson

www.cecilypaterson.com

ISBN: 978-1-942845-45-4

© Cecily Anne Paterson 2014

Second edition 2015

Printed and distributed by Ingram Spark

Distributed in Australia by Novella Distribution

www.novelladistribution.com

In memory of Mouse,
and in dedication to Katherine and Frankie,
two very cool girls who have been incredibly gracious in
allowing me to maul and overhaul their story
for my own purposes.

# AUTHOR'S NOTE

This book is set in Australia and uses Aussie words, expressions and spelling. We say 'mum' to rhyme with 'thumb'. Year 8 is the same as eighth grade and high school begins in Year 7 and goes all the way through to Year 12. We do maths, not math, and we spell analyse (and a bunch of other words) with an 's', not a 'z'. In fact, lots of our spelling is just slightly different. And, just so you know, 'the bush' is what we call the Australian forest and a 'flanny' is a checked flannelette shirt.

# PROLOGUE

My name is Coco Franks and the day after my 13th birthday, my life went nuts.

It was totally my dad's fault. And I blamed him for everything. With just three sentences he managed to completely turn my whole family upside down and ruin my life forever.

One minute we were sitting around the table about to enjoy my birthday cake. The next minute my mum was gasping, my brother was whooping, my twin sister was speechless and I was crying and running upstairs and slamming the door.

The most terrible thing about it was that finally, after a whole year of trying and hoping, my life was just about to become perfect.

But when Dad came out with his crazy idea, all I could think was this: Could things get any worse?

Ha. You'd be surprised.

# CHAPTER 1

There was a popular group in our year at school. And I don't mean just a little bit popular. I mean an uber-popular, super-elite, crazy-socialite-A-list type group. In fact, there were only two types of girl in our Year; the girls in the popular clique, and the girls who wanted to be in the popular clique. Nothing else mattered.

At primary school there had been a few kids who were kind of cool. I always seemed to know who was in or out, and my best friend Samantha and I had heaps of conversations about it (I would have talked to Charlie, my twin sister, but she was too busy playing handball to take any notice) but even if the princess-ish girls were a bit mean, no one was left as an outcast forever and mostly everyone just hung around together.

It wasn't like that at high school.

Especially not at my high school. Because, you see, from the beginning of Year Seven, Charlie didn't go to the same school as me.

People have different theories about twins. Some think you should never separate us. Others think we should be separated from kindergarten and never dressed alike or anything. And, I guess, when we got to high school, my parents must have decided that the separation theory was at least partly right. Charlie went to St Catherine's School, down the road from our house in Randwick, and I started to catch the bus — with Sam, thankfully — to St Agnes' School for boarders and day girls in the next suburb.

On the first day of Year Seven, the teachers put us into 'colour' groups to help us 'bond', whatever that was supposed to mean. There were about 15 girls in Purple with me and Samantha.

And one of them was Saffron.

The first time I saw her I just stood there and looked. I knew it was rude and I knew I looked stupid but I couldn't help it.

Saffron was truly the most beautiful person I had ever seen.

Her hair was blonde and perfectly straight. It was just messy enough to look effortless but I knew it must have taken her a long time to do it. She was tall but she didn't have that hunch that lots of tall girls have. She looked confident — almost like she was in charge of the school. Her skin was perfect and everything about her, except her nose, which, it turned out, was never, ever shiny, looked glossy and new.

She was with her friend, Tiger Lily, who was also completely beautiful but in a whole different way. Her hair was dark and she had a short, pixie haircut, white skin and pouty lips. She looked like a retro folk singer who goes on the X-Factor and wears cutesy 50s frocks with Doc Martens and bright red lipstick.

All the girls in the Purple group had to go around the circle and introduce themselves.

"Hi, I'm Susanna and I went to Bay West public school," said the first girl, smiling and looking around hopefully. She looked like she was thinking, *I really hope you like me.*

The second girl was Montana and she told us that it was her birthday in a week and giggled a bit. After that everyone did pretty much the same thing. They said their name and then a little detail about themselves and then they smiled nervously, obviously thinking, *Help me out here, people, I need some friends.*

But when it was Saffron's turn, she did it completely differently. First, she waited. It probably wasn't even a second, not long enough for anyone to really notice but just long enough so that she got everybody's attention.

"I'm Saffron," she said. Nothing else. But she didn't need anything else. She smiled and tilted her head and looked around at the group almost as if she was introducing herself to a bunch of little kids. Her eyes were big and her voice sounded sweet but at the end she gave her hair a perfect flick and all of a sudden I felt completely wrong and oddly weird. It was like I had huge hands or a pimple on my nose or massive swollen legs. My whole body seemed off-balance next to hers but I couldn't look away.

Tiger Lily was right next to her. She waited as well, but she looked back at Saffron before she spoke and raised her eyebrows.

"Tiger Lily," she said, but her voice sounded like she was making fun of us all.

The girl who was next almost couldn't get her words out.

"I'm Milly," she squeaked but no one was interested in her. Or the Sashas and Jessicas and Emilys who followed along. The only two people that were important were Saffron and Tiger and everyone wanted to be their friend.

Including me.

Because in that moment I had a revelation. Even though I sat there feeling weird and uncomfortable, I knew that I was changed forever. It's kind of cheesy, but words actually popped into my head. *This is my destiny. This is who I want to be.*

I wasn't ready yet, but I knew I could be as cool and successful as Saffron and Tiger. I could be as beautiful. I could be as stylish. This would be the area of life I could shine in.

You see, all my life I'd been number two. The second twin. Trailing along behind. Charlie was not only two minutes older than me, but she was smarter, sportier and better than me. At everything. Without even trying. She also had greener eyes, blonder hair and naturally longer eyelashes.

And after a while, it got a little bit annoying. It wasn't that I was jealous. I mean, she's my twin. I love her. It's just that it would have been nice to be number one sometimes.

The second that Saffron tossed her hair in that circle, I knew what path I was going to take in life. This would be the one thing that Charlie could never beat me at.

I was going to be popular.

Samantha had exactly the same idea.

"They are so awesome," she said to me under her breath, looking at Saffron. "So, so cool. We have to hang with them. We just have to."

There were two things stopping us. The first was the massive crush of other girls thinking the same thing and all trying to get Saffron and Tiger's attention the instant the bell went for recess. The second thing was that they already had two other friends.

Lise and Isabella were not as pretty as Saffron and Tiger but they also had perfect hair, skin, teeth and nails. All four of them wore their skirts just fractionally shorter than everyone else but not so short that they got into trouble. We watched them walk around the playground together, choose the best seats, make their way to the front of the canteen queue and completely ignore anyone who got in their way. When they walked through a crowd, a path opened up in front of them and everybody's heads turned to gaze as they went past.

But despite our best efforts and intentions, we couldn't crack it. We couldn't even figure out a way to crack it. Despite our best intentions, Sam and I had to be content with being part of a bigger group of normal girls, including squeaky Milly. We settled in to school and went to class and did our homework and got on with life.

But we were still scheming. There had to be a way to get in with Saffron and Tiger, even if it took us until we were in Year 12.

One of Samantha's strategies was to not follow their trends. I don't know if Saffron meant to deliberately start fashions but it was weird to watch it happen. One day she would wear her hat tipped back on her head slightly.

The next day 30 other girls' hats would also be tipped back. The day after that, the whole playground had their hats on a slope. When Tiger turned up at school with a new bag, 25 others had similar bags by the end of the week. When Lise got red highlights in her hair, everyone else did too.

Except for me and Samantha.

"Copying is the quickest way to be known as a nobody," Sam told me. "You've got to stay ahead, but not too far. You've got to be an individual, but not too much."

So we didn't follow the trends. But we knew exactly what they were.

About halfway through the first term of Year Seven suddenly there was a change. Shannon Davies, a girl in my English class, began to hang out with them. Samantha, who finds things out from people, had the whole story.

"Apparently they don't want an even numbered group," she said, smudging her eye liner with her finger right up close to my mirror. "Saffron likes odd numbers in a group so they picked Shannon to be the number five." She scanned the top of my dresser. It was one of those ones that are completely covered in mirror glass. It had taken me weeks to save up for it the year before and I could see about 20 different Sams reflected back at me. "Have you got any gold or silver?"

"Both. On the left, behind that tub of all those jars of nail polish," I said. "Can you see it? All the eye shadows are in that basket with the silver beads on it."

Sam chose a colour, dabbed it on and then turned

around to show me her eyelids. "What do you think Shweetie?"

"Yeah, good, Pumpkin," I said in my silly voice, but I was more interested in the Shannon thing. "Why her? I mean, she's not prettier or smarter or anything."

"I know, right?" said Samantha. "It's unfair. I mean, she's not really cool at all. Maybe she's like a sympathy project or something. Maybe they're going to give her a makeover like in the movies."

"Lucky her," I said. "I could do with a makeover." I picked up my hand mirror and examined a new zit on my chin. "I mean, look at this. It's gross," I said. And then it hit me. The numbers weren't right.

"Hang on," I said. "You said odd numbers, right? This is a problem. This means that we can never join their group together. I mean, it's basic maths. Four plus two equals six. Ba-bowww," and I made a noise like on a game show when they tell people they're out.

"Don't even say it," said Samantha. She pressed her hands against her ears dramatically. "I would do anything to be as cool as them. I so want to be popular." She put down her makeup and dropped on to my bed. I threw some gold pillows out of the way and flopped down next to her.

"I know," I said. "Me too. It's so unfair. Hey, don't crush my doona cover."

Samantha turned over towards me, smoothing out the shiny purple fabric. "I can't believe you still have purple in your room," she said.

"I knoooow," I said, half pouting. "It's just I love it so much. Obviously, I don't wear it any more. You don't have to worry about that. But I can't get rid of it." I clung in a mock-sad way to a purple cushion and made big eyes at my friend.

Sam had been kind enough to point out that purple didn't suit my skin tone after I wore a purple dress to our Year Six farewell. I had thrown out the dress the very next day, despite what Mum said, and refused to look at the photos.

"It's your choice, I guess." She wrinkled up her nose. "Anyway, have you heard about Tiger's birthday party? Apparently they're all—including Shannon—going to a day spa before the party which is, get this, on Tiger's dad's yacht, and there's going to be a DJ and everything."

"And boys too," I said. "How slack is it that we go to an all girls school! Lucky, lucky Shannon."

For the rest of the year we watched Shannon become popular and turn from normal girl to shiny princess. Her hair, face, nails and even her walk changed. Samantha and I sat on the sidelines and ached with envy. But we didn't give up. We still had big plans to be popular, even though we didn't know how it would happen.

As it turned out, it did happen. And it was all because of chocolate.

I'm lucky enough to be one of those people who doesn't really like sweet stuff. I'd rather eat sushi than lollies and snacking on brownies has never been my idea of a fun way to spend an afternoon. Tiramisu once a year on my birthday is my cake-fix limit.

But Shannon wasn't like that. She liked chocolate and sugar. A lot.

It wasn't obvious at first. When they chose her to be

part of the group, she was almost as skinny as me. But as the year went on, her bottom got bigger and bigger. I never actually saw her with a chocolate bar in her mouth, but Samantha said that apparently her bin at home was full of wrappers. You name it, she ate it.

Year Seven ended and the holidays came and went and when we got back to school, Shannon was looking chubby. Well, actually, I'll be honest. She wasn't much chubbier than most people in our Year. In fact if you met her for the first time, you would probably say she was normal sized, but in comparison to the year before, she'd put on heaps of weight.

And it was too much for Saffron, Tiger, Lise and Isabella. At the end of week five, they dropped her, and they dropped her hard. One day she was walking around the playground with them, and the next she was sitting on a bench on her own with a red face, looking like she'd been crying.

I felt sorry for her. We were back in English together and on the third day after she had been dropped she was still crying. The word had got around the school that no one was supposed to talk to her or Tiger would have something to say to them. She was on her own.

But when someone sitting opposite you is crying in class, it doesn't really matter about all that. You want to give them a hand, right?

Besides, it was safe that day. None of the popular girls were in the same class as us and even Sam, who I knew wouldn't have approved of me being nice to Shannon, just because it went against what Tiger had said, was away.

"Are you okay?" I whispered when the teacher turned around.

Shannon looked up, surprised. She sniffed and then looked helplessly around her so I dug in my bag for a tissue. It was a bit crumpled but it was still unused and she didn't seem to mind.

"Thanks," she said and gave me a weak smile but her eyes were welling up again, so I pulled the whole packet out and put it on her desk.

From that point on, whenever I saw her, I gave her a secret smile. I wasn't quite brave enough to do it openly and go against Saffron and Tiger Lily but it seemed a bit sad that someone should have no friends in the whole world so I did what I could.

Samantha had absolutely no sympathy for her at all.

"Well it's her own fault," she said. "If she wasn't so piggish, she wouldn't have got so fat and then she wouldn't have got dropped. I mean, it's simple. You keep your mouth shut if you don't want to put on weight. She must've known what would happen."

I nodded. When you put it like that, of course it was true, but the part of me that loves kittens and puppies still felt sorry for Shannon and I wasn't about to tell Samantha. She was busy obsessing about who was going to replace Shannon.

Because Saffron and Tiger were holding auditions.

# CHAPTER 2

First, the word went around our year. Milly told Emily who told Breeanna who told Brittnee. Soon everyone knew. "Tiger said they're definitely going to choose someone else to join them, but only one person."

"Really? Only one?"

"Definitely only one."

No one could stop talking about it. Hayley, a girl whose dad was a bookmaker at the races was even taking odds on who it might be. Sam drove me crazy. She was on the phone for three hours one night going through all the names.

"It might be Leigh, but she's probably not cool enough. You know how she wears her bag, always about to drop off her shoulder. I think they'd think she's a bit too messy. It could be you. But probably not. Because, you know, you'd have to get your teeth fixed."

I slid my tongue around my mouth. My teeth were definitely a problem. It wasn't that they stuck out or anything. It wasn't even that I had braces. It's just that for some unknown reason my enamel was stained.

Samantha first pointed it out when I was eleven and

I made a decision to never smile in a photograph again until they were fixed. When Mum noticed my closed lips in every picture she wanted to know what was going on.

"It's really not that bad, Coco," she said, staring into my mouth. "I mean, the colour is a little bit uneven, I guess. Maybe over here a bit. But it's no worse than anyone else."

When I cried, she looked again and then compared with Charlie's teeth.

"Well, I suppose there is a bit of difference," she said after about five minutes.

"Yeah, but really?" said Charlie. "Is it that much of a problem?"

I stamped my foot.

"Seriously, you'd have to be blind not to notice how ugly they are. I really need to get them fixed. Please let me? Please!"

"Okay," said Mum. She said it in that way that people do when they're kind of giving up and giving in. "Oh-kaaaay. I'll talk to the dentist and we'll see what they can do. It's not the kind of thing that you should get done before you're a teenager though. You'll have to wait until you're at least thirteen."

Thirteen was this year. And I had plans. But they would still have to wait just a little longer, because Samantha hadn't actually stopped talking yet.

"It might be Georgia, except have you seen how she's dip-dyed her hair? Probably not. Maybe Savannah. I mean, she's pretty and she's tall and she's smart, but not too smart if you know what I mean... I'm not saying she's dumb, right? She's just not a brain box nerd."

"Sam, I've got to go to bed," I said eventually. "My mum's going to come up here and take the phone out of my hand if you don't get off. We can talk about it tomorrow. Just try to get some sleep, okay?"

We'd all been going nuts for a week before Saffron and Tiger picked about five people they thought possibly might be good enough and wrote each person a little note, inviting them to have a 'conversation' over lunch.

Samantha and I both got notes. We were both ecstatic.

"You see?" she said. "My strategy worked. We didn't follow too closely, but we didn't separate off from the group too much. They can see that we're individuals, but not like, crazy individuals. How are we going to do our hair? It will have to be perfect. This is it. This really is it. This is make or break for us."

I still had a question in my head about odd numbers and even numbers and two of us and four of them but I didn't say it out loud. Perhaps Saffron would see what great friends Samantha and I were and pick both of us. Anyway, I had other things to think about, including my teeth and how I would have to be careful not to smile too much.

On the day of my 'conversation' I had to go over to their seat by myself and answer questions from all four of them about things like clothes and music and shoe designers. Samantha had spent the whole week reading recent copies of fashion and gossip magazines and she had tried about twenty different hairdos over the weekend before she finally settled on one that to me looked just like Saffron's messy, straight do. I wasn't going to tell her so though. She'd already panicked for about seventy-two hours straight.

She panicked for another seventy-two hours while the girls made their decision. By the end of those three days Charlie was giving me grief at home.

"Auditions? To become a member of a group?" She was incredulous. "Are they for real? What's so special about them anyway?"

I got defensive. "Just because you don't care about these things doesn't mean they aren't important," I said. "These girls are like the pinnacle of Year Eight. Everyone wants to be like them. If I get to be in the group, that's pretty much my social life sorted out for the rest of high school. I'll be the best there is. I mean, it's all just basically a competition, right? If I get in, I'll have won."

"Unless you get too fat, of course," she said, raising one eyebrow at me. I tried to raise mine back at her, but my face failed and she burst out laughing. I screwed up my nose at her. At least I could do that. It's so unfair. How come some people can raise an eyebrow and others can't?

"But seriously," I said, flopping myself over on the patchwork quilt on Charlie's bed. "I don't think they'll pick me anyway. Not being vain or anything, but I'm too pretty to be their makeover kind of project, and being realistic, other people know more about fashion and stuff than me so they will probably choose them." I thought for a minute. "It would be the coolest birthday present ever though…"

Yes, Charlie and I were going to turn 13 in a week's time. But what I hadn't told her was that if I was picked, I'd have to go to a day spa with Saffron and the whole group on the actual day of our birthday.

I wasn't going to mention it before I had to. Charlie would be upset if she thought that I was hoping to do something else on our birthday. Every single year for twelve years we'd woken up together, opened our presents together and had a party together. I wasn't looking forward to possibly telling her that I wanted to go away with my potential new friends.

But that's exactly what I had to do.

Because, miraculously, somehow I made it in.

# CHAPTER 3

I got the note in second period history, slipped to me by Isabella across the aisle. She smiled as she gave it to me and my tummy went to jelly. In the background Mrs Corrington was droning on about ancient Egypt but I couldn't listen. I held the note in both hands, took a deep breath and then opened it all in one movement.

The paper was the creamiest, smoothest paper I'd ever touched, with black curly designs all around the edge. At the bottom someone had stuck on five tiny pale pink love hearts stickers, and in a hot pink pen, Saffron's handwriting read:

Dear Coco,
You are officially invited to join our group. You're one of us! Come sit with us at lunch.
Saffron, Tiger Lily, Isabella, Lise

My heart skipped a beat. I blinked and blinked again. Was this real? I felt like Charlie Bucket from that kids' movie, holding his golden ticket, except that (obviously) mine was pink and black.

"It's happened!" I breathed quietly to myself. "I'm popular. This is it."

It felt amazing. I wanted to jump up and down like a little kid and yell, "I won, I won! I'm the king of the castle!" It took everything I had to keep control of myself and act cool and sophisticated. When I finally got to go off to the bathroom with Samantha, I let out a little bit of the squealing that had been piling up inside.

"Me! Me! They picked me! Can you believe it?" I yelped, grabbing her shoulder and bouncing on my toes, pushing the note in her face. She pushed me off.

"Ow! Stop it. You're on my foot," she said. And then she smiled. "It's amazing! I mean really amazing. I never really thought that they would pick you. There are other people who are skinnier than you, or taller, and — no offence or anything — cooler than you. I mean, even my hair is longer than yours, and of course, your teeth... So yeah, it is amazing."

I looked at her face and suddenly got a shock. She was completely jealous.

"Oh Sam," I said, my smile crumbling. "I'm really sorry. You wanted this just as much as I did, I know. Do you want me to tell them no?"

She looked at me like she couldn't believe what she'd just heard. "Are you crazy? If you say no you'll be sitting on the bench with Shannon and I'll be back at the end of the queue as well. No way. You have to do this."

"Really?" I said. "You're so sweet. We'll be in this together. You can help me! You can coach me. I'll need your help. We'll get together every day and debrief."

"Definitely," she said. "I mean, I've already been

coaching you for ages." She twisted her face. "Seriously, this only happened because of me. If you hadn't followed the strategies, they probably wouldn't even have looked at you. So you can't forget me or leave me behind."

"Of course I won't," I said, soothing her. "I'll do this for you and me. If I get an opportunity to invite you to a party or something — anything, I will. I know you'd do the same for me."

And that was the way my life as one of the most popular girls in the school began, with four new friends in front of me and an old friend behind me, backing me up.

The first thing I did with Saffron, Tiger, Isabella and Lise was take some photos. We put our heads together, pursed up our lips and went click click click on our phones (although in my case, it was an iPod. Mum still had to be talked into letting me have an actual phone. Something about me having to be able to afford to pay the bills. Whatever. It was annoying.)

"Beautiful!" gushed Lise, looking at one of the side of my face. "Ears!"

"She thinks you have beautiful ears," said Isabella.

"Really?" I said, touching my earlobe. I had never ever noticed my ears before.

"No, no, it's your eyes and your lips. That's why you're so pretty," said Saffron sweetly. "You're so gorgeous. You're amazing."

For the rest of the day I kept pulling my iPod out under my desk. I couldn't stop looking at our photos. Saffron, of course, was in the middle of them all. She was still as pretty as the first day I saw her, with her blonde and perfectly straight hair, blue eyes and perfect skin, but she wasn't so much pretty as just completely elegant. She had gotten taller since Year Seven, and her legs looked about twice as long as mine. It was all the little details, like today's tiny peasant style braid in her hair and the vintage designer floral bag she carried, that really made the difference though. Nothing looked wrong. Not ever. Saffron was as perfect as you could get.

Samantha, who always knew, told me that Saffron's family was so rich that they had a holiday house in Palm Beach and an apartment in Paris as well as one in New York. There was even a rumour around that they owned a tropical island. Apparently Saffron's dad was in charge of a whole bank or something so there was plenty of cash. She probably could have afforded to go to one of the even more exclusive schools around our area but Samantha (and again, I had no idea how she found this stuff out) said that her dad was a 'self-made man' (whatever that means) and that he wanted her to come to St Agnes to 'meet real people'.

Saffron was smiling in most of the photographs, but Tiger Lily wasn't. Her face was more about the attitude than the smile. She had big green eyes and the blackest, longest eyelashes you've ever seen without mascara. She must have gotten them dyed — like her hair, which was currently a dark auburn red with black streaks, but it looked cool and not trashy because she had a great cut. Everything about her was edgy and urban and tough. I couldn't imagine her next to a cow or in a field of flowers. She would have looked completely wrong.

When Tiger started school, it went around that her

mum was the editor of Snap! Magazine, which everyone reads all the time. I even went out and bought a copy just to check if the surnames were the same — and it was true. In the first few days a lot of people asked Tiger to get her mum's autograph or free copies of Snap! but Tiger is pretty much like her name and I don't think too many people asked again.

Isabella and Lise were as different from each other as anyone can be. Isabella was Italian, with black hair and olive skin, whereas Lise was Scandinavian-white-blonde with big, blue puppy dog eyes. Lise's parents were both artists and her dad won an award last year for some painting competition, which I only knew about because my mum was reading about it in the newspaper. She looked up and said, "Isn't there a girl at your school with this surname? I think I met her mum at a lunch once."

Isabella's parents were solicitors and she had three younger brothers who she didn't like at all. While we were taking selfies she got really mad when she discovered a bunch of pictures on her phone of her brothers with their mouths gaping wide open.

"They've been playing on my phone again," she said. "It's so annoying. I'm going to have to get a lock on my door. I can't stand it when they do this. I mean, little brothers are the worst. You just have no idea what they're going to wreck next. I just tell my mum that she should keep them under control but she rolls her eyes and yells at me instead. I mean, is that fair?"

Tiger raised an eyebrow. "Just put a pass code on the phone," she said.

"I did that before but they managed to get me to tell

them what it was. I have no idea how they did it. They think they can make me say anything." Isabella said. She passed her phone to Lise, who scrolled through the pictures.

"Brothers!" she said.

That first day it took me a while to get used to being looked at all the time. I followed along as the other girls sashayed around the playground and I could hear my name being whispered through every class. A couple of times, when I heard something like, "why her?" my face would start to go red but I gave myself a talking-to.

"Social stuff and popularity is my thing. It's what I'm good at and I deserve it. Anyway, if Charlie can win everything else, I can win this." Then I tried to channel some of Charlie's effortless confidence and immediately felt better.

After two days I got used to it. I loved that everyone was looking at me. I loved the feeling of being on top and I loved having Saffron smile at me and hearing even Tiger Lily say something complimentary.

The only thing I didn't love was telling Charlie and Mum that we had to put off our birthday celebrations.

"You're kidding, right?" said Charlie, taking a sip of her drink. We were sitting at the back of the house, looking onto our long, terrace garden. Her face was puzzled. "You want to go to some spa thing all day with people you hardly know on our birthday? Why can't they just change the day? Why do you have to go anyway?"

"You know about this. I explained to you about these girls," I said. "It's part of being in the group, going to the things they organise. If I don't go, it's going to look like I don't really want to be friends with them and they might drop me when they've only just picked me. It's too much of a risk not to go. Please. At least try to understand!"

"It seems a little bit extreme," said Mum. She had a cup of tea in front of her and was nibbling on carrot sticks and pesto. "They can't be very nice friends if they'd drop someone because they can't go out with them one day. Are you sure that they're the sort of girls you really want to hang around with?"

"They're fine, Mum," I said, a little bit between my teeth. I picked up a piece of carrot and crunched. "F-i-i-ine. Seriously. You don't get it. Please, it won't really matter if we have a birthday dinner on Sunday instead. I mean, it's just a day, right? The important thing is that we celebrate it. I mean, half the people in the world don't even know the exact date they're born on, and they still have birthdays."

"That's the stupidest argument I ever heard of," said Charlie. She was tipping back on her chair and looked sulky. "Mum, this is ridiculous."

I tried a different tack. "Well, do you remember three years ago when Charlie made it to State for freestyle and the competition day was on our birthday? And you had to go to Canberra and you weren't back until late so we had our cake and party on the next day instead? This is kind of the same thing."

Mum looked thoughtful. She slurped her tea. "But it's not really sport," she said. "I mean, this is a bit different."

"Yes, but I don't do sport," I said. Under the table I clenched my fingers in frustration. "I'm never going to be in a sports competition like Charlie. Not a serious one anyway. You know that. It's not really fair if Charlie gets to change the days because of sport but because I don't play sport I don't get to! This is social stuff and fashion stuff—this is what I'm good at. This is what matters to me. Isn't that as important as a sports competition?"

Mum looked almost convinced. Maybe I should have been in the debating team after all. "Well, I guess if you put it like that... Maybe just this once we could change the day, if Charlie agrees?"

Charlie looked like she was coming around as well. "Alright," she said. It was a long drawn out one. "But you still have to sing to me in the morning when we get up."

"I'll sing as loud as I possibly can," I said, smiling. "Thank you, Mum, thank you, thank you."

"Thank Charlie as well," she said so I burst into a terrible rendition of 'You are my sunshine' which is what I always sing to her on our birthday, complete with cheesy actions. I've been doing it for four years now. It's what Mum used to sing to us both when we shared a room when we were little. We have a love/hate relationship with Mum's voice so it's fun to take her off. She doesn't realise that she sings off-key.

"Ha ha," said Charlie. "Thank you—not! Have fun on your silly spa day. But you'd better come back extra beautiful or I won't let you do it again."

# CHAPTER 4

It sounds kind of crazy now that I think about it but sitting around in towels with four other girls in a day spa all covered in mud, with gunk on our faces and cucumber slices on our eyes, was the most sophisticated and cool I had ever felt in my life.

I had felt slightly grossed out at the beginning when the woman started to smooth out the mud all over my shoulders and neck. *Icky, icky icky!* I thought. But I tried to calm down and be cool. Mud might not be my thing, but I was doing this to be popular. Plus the most exclusive girls in the school were being really nice to me.

"So is it actually your birthday today?" said Saffron, smiling.

"Yup," I said. "And my sister as well. Thirteen today!"

"Sister?" asked Lise, picking off her cucumber slices and looking at me with surprise. "How?"

"Um, they're twins?" said Tiger Lily, giving her a look.

"Oh," said Lise. "Twins!" Her big blue eyes looked like they were about to fall out of her face.

"Can you, like, read each other's thoughts?" said

Isabella. "Isn't it like if you pinch one twin, the other one feels the pain? Because I've got cousins who are twins and when one of them broke her arm the other one had to go to hospital as well… "

"I think that's more identical twins," I said. "We don't look exactly like each other. We're more like sisters born at the same time."

"Oh, I know what that is. It's a funny word, I'm trying to think of it… Oh I know — fraternal. You guys are fraternal twins, right?" said Isabella. "Is that the word for it?"

"Whatever. Happy birthday," said Tiger Lily, just slightly rolling her eyes.

"We got you something," said Saffron and she delicately turned around and pulled out a pink and white striped package with a black bow. I tried to take it without getting mud from my fingers on the paper. I didn't know whether to open it or not but Saffron was looking at me expectantly so I pulled the paper apart gently to find a very expensive box of chocolates.

I tried to look enthusiastic, even though I don't particularly like chocolates. "Oh, thanks a lot!" I said, but I could feel Tiger Lily's eyes in my back.

"Are you going to have one?" she said and she raised her eyebrows slightly.

"Would you like one?" I said and I offered them out to her.

"No thanks," she said, so I passed it to Isabella and Lise instead.

"No!" declared Lise.

"Not for me, thanks, not today," said Isabella, darting

a look at Tiger Lily and then shaking her head as well. There was only one person left—Saffron—so I offered one to her.

"No," she said sweetly. "I don't eat chocolate. It makes me fat," and she smiled again and tossed her head.

For a second I didn't know what to think. Why would they give me chocolates but then refuse to have any? I suddenly felt nervous and chewed on my lips. What was going on? I put them down behind me. "I'll take them home and give some to my sister," I said.

And then something very surprising happened. Lise started to giggle. And then Saffron and Isabella joined in. It took a few seconds before Tiger Lily smiled but when she did, she almost looked happy. I was still confused.

"You see?" said Saffron. "I told you so." She looked around at the others as if to say *I was right.* Then she sat up and, with a big smile on her face, stuck out her hand to congratulate me.

"Welcome our group, Coco. You've passed the first test," she said.

My eyes went wide. For a second I felt sick.

"The chocolates were a test?" I said.

"Yes. And you've passed. We needed to make sure you weren't going to pig out on them."

I gasped. "Nice one. That was good," I said, trying to look amused and cool. "I haven't liked chocolate since I was three years old. It just doesn't do it for me."

"You're so lucky!" said Isabella. "I love it so much, it's so yummy... but we don't eat it." She sounded wistful.

"At all. Ever." Tiger Lily came into the conversation. It sounded like a warning.

"No," smiled Saffron. "And in fact, one reason we got you to come here today away from school and everything, Coco, is because we need to tell you the rules."

"Rules?" I said, trying to get the alarm out of my voice and sound casual.

"Yes," said Tiger Lily. "Rules. It's pretty simple. We're the top of the pile. I'm not being arrogant. I'm just stating a fact. We know we're at the top and we're going to stay there." She waved her hand around as if to say, *See how beautiful we are? This just doesn't all happen by chance.* "The rules set the standard. If you break them, you get dropped."

"Okay," I said. "Um. That sounds... fair."

Saffron came back into the conversation. "It's not because we're worried about *you,*" she smiled. I felt a little relieved. "It's because of what happened with Shannon. Basically, we want you, but you have to know that things can change."

"Sure, sure, I get it," I said, nodding my head off. "Just tell me what the rules are. It'll be cool."

I probably should have gone home and written up the rules that night on a fluorescent piece of cardboard with a massive great thick marker pen and then stuck them in the middle of my mirror so that I could see them every day, twice a day when I brushed my hair and put on my makeup. It would have saved me a lot of tears and a whole lot of disaster further down the track. But, as Mum says all the time, you only know what you know at the time you know it.

These were the rules of the most exclusive group in my school, told to me that day in the spa by Tiger Lily.

These were the rules that I was to break at my own peril:

1.    We always look good. ("No!" chimed in Lise. "Perfect!")

2.    We don't get fat. ("No chocolate or chips," mourned Isabella. "Or chocolate chips either." She giggled at her own joke.)

3.    We don't associate with losers. ("We don't talk to losers, we don't look at losers, we don't flirt with losers, we don't go out with losers," said Tiger Lily.)

4.    There are no secrets. (This is where Saffron spoke up, opening her big blue eyes wide. "We can't risk our reputations. We don't want to get surprised if we hear about something you've done that might make us look bad. What you do is our business now that you're in our group. Soooo," and she shrugged her shoulders, "we need you to be completely honest.")

5.    There are consequences for breaking the rules. (Here no one said anything. Isabella looked scared, Lise looked down, Saffron looked superior and Tiger Lily just looked at me full in the face, narrowing her eyes.)

At the end of it I was breathing faster and my head was spinning. This wasn't going to be as simple as I thought. What if I forgot the rules? What if I accidentally did my hair wrong one day? What if I made a fashion faux pas? What if I talked to someone I shouldn't talk to without realising it? Would they just drop me immediately or would I get a chance to make it up? And what were the consequences? Was I even game enough to ask?

The panic must have started to show on my face because Saffron came over to sit next to me.

"Don't worry," she said. "I picked you for a reason.

You're different from the other, ordinary girls. You're one of us. You belong here."

I smiled bravely. "Thanks. I'm so glad I'm here. You have no idea. It's really cool." I shrugged. I didn't really know what else to say. "I'll try my best."

Saffron's face was warm and welcoming. "You know, you're really pretty," she said. "But you should do your hair like this sometimes," and she scraped and pulled my hair into the highest ponytail ever. "Oh wow — that's great. Hey girls, what do you think of this?"

"That looks heaps better," said Isabella quickly. "That really suits your face, Coco. You should wear it like that all the time. It looks amazing, just like the way the model had it in that magazine I saw last week... what was its name? Sparkle? Spangle? Something like that..."

Saffron cut her off. "You could probably get it to be shinier, which would help. I'll show you the shampoo that I use. It's exclusive. You can only get it from the salon I go to and it's really expensive but it's so worth it."

When we washed off the mud and the face gunk the conversation changed from being all about me to being all about people I'd never heard of. I focused on listening hard, trying to get used to everything and learning a whole lot of new names.

"Remember that girl Cecelia who was in Year Five with us?" said Isabella. "The one whose brother was school captain? Well my mum said that they've moved out of Sydney."

"Where to?" said Tiger Lily. "Melbourne? Please don't say Paris or New York or something amazing like that."

"No, no," said Isabella. "Nothing cool. Nothing cool

at all. It was like out in the back of beyond or something. They moved to somewhere like Tamworth or Wagga or something. Out there—you know." And she waved a hand behind her.

"Country?" said Lise. She stared dreamily in front of her. "Cows! Cute!"

Tiger Lily looked at her and rolled her eyes. "Cows stink and they do very big poos," she said. She turned to Isabella. "Why did they go there? There's nothing out there. How is she going to have a social life? Some parents are just stupid."

"I know, right?" said Isabella. "But what's even worse is that she's going to some local public high school. So sad. She was quite nice."

"Loserville," said Tiger Lily. "You can't come back from that, no matter how pretty you are or whatever. She's stuck in Loserville." She shook her head. "I would kill my mum if she ever moved out of the city. Actually, I just wouldn't go. And I'd like to see anyone try and make me."

"Let's talk about something else," said Saffron, getting impatient. "We're breaking our own rules—even talking about losers. Let's talk about someone heaps more interesting." She gave me a secretive smile and winked.

"Oh yes, yes, yes!" giggled Lise, just about jumping up and down. "Tell her!"

I must've looked worried again because Saffron immediately tried to calm me down.

"It's okay," she said. "It's just that we've got someone who we really want you to meet." Lise gave a chortle of joy and even Tiger looked animated.

"Who is it?" I said. Was it another friend of theirs? A hairdresser? A manicurist? I was confused.

"Well, he's sixteen, he's a friend of my brother, he goes to St Vincent's School and he's really good looking," said Saffron, smiling.

I blushed. "A boy?" I said. "Cool."

"Oh, believe me, he is," said Tiger. "Cool, that is." She looked at me. "If I wasn't already going out with Toby, I'd consider him."

"Do you already have a boyfriend?" I asked. I guess I should have expected it.

Tiger looked at me like I was stupid. "Of course," she said. "We all do."

"Well, kind of, anyway," said Isabella. "Saffron goes out with Ed. He's in Year 10 and he does rowing."

"Muscles!" said Lise, grinning.

Isabella swatted her on the head. "Tiger goes out with Toby—they've been together for ages. I have a boyfriend in Brisbane—kind of—but I still flirt with a guy called Danny, and Lise won't decide between Soapy and Foggo." She looked at my surprised face. "Nicknames. Soapy is Sam and Foggo is Zac Fogarty. Get it? Oh, and they're all pretty much friends of each other."

"Are they all, like, older?" I asked.

"Of course," said Saffron. "I mean, have you seen any Year Eight boys recently?" She made a face and rolled her eyes.

"Ick!" agreed Lise.

"We only talk to guys in Year 10 and up," said Tiger. "We don't bother with babies."

"But anyway," said Saffron. "The point is that we're

glad you're here because Ed and Toby have a new friend called Darcy. We met him in the holidays and he is really good looking."

"Mmm. Dark hair, nice shoulders," said Isabella, nodding. "He's a rower, isn't he? Doesn't he row with the guys? Isn't he in the same boat?"

"Anyway," said Saffron, ignoring Isabella, "he told us to find him someone — just like you really. He likes long hair and a cute face."

"He said that he trusts Saffron to find him the perfect girl!" said Isabella. "How romantic is that?"

I could feel my face going pink and prickly all over. This was completely awesome as well as being utterly embarrassing. But his name was a good start. I'd been in love with Mr Darcy from Pride and Prejudice ever since Mum first showed me the TV series. And if Saffron liked him, he must be extremely cool.

"So, what's he like?" I asked.

"What?" said Tiger, looking at me oddly. "We just told you. Dark hair, good looking, rower, goes to school at St Vincent's. What else do you need?"

"His dad is really rich — does that help?" said Isabella. "And his family goes skiing every year in the US." She looked confused, like she didn't really understand the question. I didn't know how to tell her that I was talking about whether he had a sense of humour and if he was quiet or loud. Things like that. But Saffron came to the rescue.

"Here, this is what he's like," she said and she pulled out her phone. "I've got a photo of him and Ed. You can have a look."

She passed the phone over to me and I nearly died on the spot. There on the screen was a photograph of the most beautiful boy I had ever seen in my life. He had dark curly hair, olive skin, black eyes and a smile that I couldn't take my eyes off.

Before that minute I'd never understood books or poems that talked about things like hearts melting or people going weak at the knees, but as soon as I saw that photograph I felt both of those things at once. If I hadn't been sitting down, I might have fallen over. As it was I had to catch my breath and control my voice.

"Wow," I said, my eyes opening wide. And that was all I could say.

"She likes him!" said Isabella. "Look at her face. She's in love! Woo hoo!"

"Crush!" said Lise.

Even Tiger Lily lifted her eyes in amusement to Saffron who gave me a great big smile. "See, I knew you'd like him."

It was true. I liked Darcy, just from one photograph. And having seen how he looked, suddenly I didn't even care about if he had a sense of humour or what his personality or his character was like or anything. I just wanted to go out with him. Besides, if someone was so good looking, surely they'd just have to be nice as well, right? My heart was gone and I hadn't even met him yet.

"The best part is that he's looking for someone just like you," said Saffron. "I know. Let's take your picture right now and send it to him."

Before I had time to say anything, the four of them were fussing around me, wiping off stray bits of mud, fixing my hair and even putting on some make-up that they had whipped out of their bags. In two minutes flat I was photo ready and Saffron was standing in front of me with her phone saying, "Come on Coco, give me a good pose."

I smiled as nicely as I could but she just laughed. "No, a real pose. Look at Lise." I turned to see Lise with her shoulders lowered, her head to one side and her lips all pouty. "Like that."

I felt awkward but I tried and when Saffron had taken the picture she showed it to me. "Not bad," she said, "but you have to practice in the mirror when you get home. Are you ready? I'm going to send it to him."

My stomach jumped a little bit and I felt embarrassed but everyone was crowded around the phone so they didn't notice. It only took about twenty seconds before Saffron's phone buzzed with an answer. The girls squealed.

"It's him, it's him!" bounced Isabella, jumping up and down. "What did he say? What did he say?"

Saffron shook them off and cleared a space. She looked at me with a knowing smile. "Do you want to hear it?" she asked me.

I nodded, trying to smile over my nervous tummy.

"Ahem. So, I texted 'this is Coco. What do you think? Want to meet?' And he wrote back—get ready for this—'Hot. Keep her for me.'" She gave me a great big smile. "He likes you!"

"Wow. Can I see?" I said. Her phone felt smooth in my hand. I read the message again, just to be sure. Maybe, just maybe, I'd have an actual boyfriend soon, just like Saffron and Tiger.

"I know, she should send him a message," said Tiger.

"No, I don't think so... not yet," I said, handing back the phone quickly. "I haven't even met him."

Tiger smiled wickedly. "No, no, you should," she said. And she grabbed the phone from Saffron and started to text. "Here, I'll do it for you." She started pressing buttons while I stood there, unable to move.

"How's this? 'Hi Darcy. It's Coco. How RU?'" She pressed the send button and looked at me, an amused expression on her face. The phone buzzed in her hand about a second later.

"Oops," said Tiger. "It's for you!" She handed me the phone back and as I read the message my face went completely red.

'Hey. Nice smile. I like blue eyes.'

"You have to answer him now," she said happily. "What are you going to say?"

I took the phone awkwardly and texted the only thing I could think of which was, 'thanks'. Tiger Lily made a face when she saw it. "Is that all you've got? Seriously?"

"Give her a break, Tiger," said Saffron. "She's probably never texted a boy before in her life. Oh, there it goes again," she said. "He's replying."

The phone buzzed and there was another message from Darcy. 'We shd meet up some time.'

Before Tiger had a chance to read the message, I replied with 'okay' and handed the phone back to Saffron. "Sorry," I said, jumping up and down a little and pretending to be desperate. "I just really need to go to the loo."

I had to escape and a toilet break is sometimes a girl's best friend. I sat in the cubicle for longer than I needed and took a few deep breaths before heading back in. Clearly, things moved quickly around here. If that had been Samantha and me, we would have giggled about Darcy for months and looked at his picture a hundred times before we even thought about getting up the courage to actually talk to him. I felt breathless, not just because he was gorgeous and I had a crush on him, but because everything was moving so fast.

When I finally came back in, Saffron and Tiger were still texting Darcy, giggling every so often.

"He says he wants to meet you, but he's going overseas for six weeks the day after tomorrow, so he can't do it before that. But when he gets back, it's for sure." Saffron smiled at me. "He really thinks you're cute."

I breathed a secret sigh of relief. There would be time to get used to the whole idea.

Of course, I didn't realise then that I wouldn't be around in six weeks. How could I have even guessed that the very next day, everything was going to go completely and utterly crazy?

# CHAPTER 5

I made sure I sang to Charlie again when I got home. She and Josh (yes, he's my annoying older brother) gave me the usual amount of teasing but she said she'd missed me and I said the same to her, so we were okay with each other. I tried to be generous to Josh, given that I was now popular and sophisticated, and ignored him with great dignity for about half an hour but he made one too many cracks about my new hairstyle so I had to hit him and then I ended up cleaning the toilet, which is Mum's usual punishment for fighting, despite the fact that it was my birthday.

I went off to bed cranky and tired from the day spa (who knew relaxing could be so exhausting?) but everything's better after a good night's sleep and the next day we were ready to celebrate properly. The usual stuff happened; Charlie and I gave each other presents (lipstick for me from Charlie, yoga pants for Charlie from me), we had pancakes for breakfast, we fielded about five phone calls from aunts and grandmas and then we got to choose what we'd do for the day, which of course was to go to the beach. I sat on the sand and sunbaked while Charlie headed out on her surfboard with Dad and Josh. In the afternoon we listened to music and chilled out while Dad said he had to go out and sign some papers or something, and then we were ready for the big event—dinner and cake!

Mum put up the decorations like she does every time we have a family celebration. She made some bunting out of red and orange material a few years ago and it comes out for every birthday or special occasion. Mum likes to celebrate stuff. When we were little she bought red plates especially for the birthday person. She also brings them out if one of us wins a prize or a trophy for something. Charlie has eaten off a lot of red plates over the years.

"What are we having to eat?" asked Charlie. "Is it roast?" Roast lamb is her favourite food, followed by chocolate pudding and ice cream. I like it too, but I'm more of a Thai food kind of girl. I like to think it's a little bit more exotic.

"Don't worry," said Mum, poking her head around the kitchen door, "I've done favourites for everyone." She was fussing around in the kitchen putting food on plates. "Josh, come in here and help me bring out the food please."

Josh snorted and groaned and unfolded himself from the table where he was already sitting down. "It's so unfair—I have to be the only slave when it's their birthday. At least when it's my birthday there are two of them to help each other."

"But you love us so much," said Charlie. "You can't wait to do the washing up on our birthday. Go on, admit it. You've been hanging out for this all year."

"You, I love," said Josh, pointing at Charlie on his way to the kitchen. "Her, I'm not so sure about." He nodded his head towards me.

"What?" I yelped. I actually felt hurt. "What's wrong with me? You can't just love her and not me. That's not fair. Anyway, we're twins. You have to love us both."

"Yeah, well I would, except you look stupid," said Josh, coming back with a dish in his hands. "I mean, what is that?" He pointed to my forehead. "It looks like you've got a huge green pimple."

I put my hand up to my head and fingered the stick-on jewel that I had carefully placed on my forehead especially for dinner.

"It's a bindi, you moron," I said. "It's supposed to make me beautiful. It's Indian." I rolled my eyes. "Didn't you know? The whole Bollywood look is really big right now." Tiger had worn one to the day spa and it looked so good on her I just had to try it out.

"Well, you look ridiculous," said Josh. "I guess that's pretty normal for you though."

I made a noise of frustration and lunged at him from across the table. Charlie put her hand up to catch the dish of potatoes he was carrying. "Watch out, Coco," she said. "You nearly spilled it all."

Mum stuck her head around the door frame. "Coco!" she said. "Stop it, you three. Can't you get on once in a blue moon? And especially on your birthday! Stop fighting. And does anyone know where Dad is? I heard him come in but I haven't seen him yet."

"I'll go and look for him," I said, pleased to have a

reason to get away. As I left the dining room I turned around and stuck my tongue out at Josh. He made a face at me and said, "Later... "

I skipped out into the hallway.

"Dad!" I called. The sound echoed up and down the corridor and the staircases. Our house was big, old and three stories high. Dad could have been anywhere. I headed down the hallway.

"Dad! Dinner is ready. You have to come now. Mum says so."

There was a rustle and a creak from Dad's study. I tapped on the door and stuck my head around. "Dad, are you in there? Did you hear me? Dinner's ready. Are you coming?"

He looked up guiltily from the sofa, where he seemed to be stuffing a stack of papers back into his briefcase. "Yes, I know. I'll be there in just a second. I just have to sort this out and then I'll come."

I ran back down the hall to the dining room and slid into my seat again. Josh had forgotten his persecution of my bindi and was now busy punching Charlie in the arm. A minute later Dad walked in. Out of the corner of my eye I could see that he had brought in his briefcase. He had a look on his face like he was squashing down something big. A flash of curiosity passed through my mind but then Mum had the food on the table and we were all sitting down, saying grace and eating and eating and eating.

"That was the best ever," said Charlie, leaning back and rubbing her belly. "I am so full."

"Well, you'd better leave room for cake," said Mum,

pushing out her chair and getting ready to leave the table. "It's tiramisu."

Tiramisu is definitely my favourite cake in the world, and my mum makes it amazingly. Whenever I eat it I tell her I think she should go on a cooking show on TV, but she just laughs and shakes her head. "I don't cook for judges," she always says. "I cook for fun."

But it wasn't quite time for tiramisu just yet.

"No, no," I said. "It's always presents before cake." We have a tradition in our family where there is always an extra present before the birthday cake as well as the ones in the morning.

Mum reached around to a bag behind the door. "You're right," she said, handing me a pink package with a fluffy bow on it, and Charlie a green and white spotted parcel with a brown bow. "Happy birthday, girls," she said.

Dad nodded. "Happy birthday."

We both started opening. I like to do it carefully whereas Charlie just rips into the paper but we still manage to get to the gift part at the same time. When we were little, we always got identical gifts. Auntie Jo would always give us matching clothes and Uncle Peter usually found us a book each in the same series. It kind of took the surprise out of Christmas morning or birthday parties, so we worked out that if we opened the presents from the same people at the same time, we could both enjoy it together. Even though now our parents and our friends have worked out that yes, we are actually pretty different, and it's probably a good idea to buy us different things, we still have a habit of opening up together.

"It's the skinny jeans I wanted," I yelled in delight. And then Charlie screamed, "A riding helmet!" She looked to Mum and Dad for an explanation.

"We've been looking at those horse pictures you've been pasting up on your walls all year," said Mum. (It was true. Charlie had liked horses since she was really young but it had upped a notch this year when she started collecting horse books and pictures and putting them everywhere.)

"We thought if you really want to ride that much, we would arrange some lessons this year," said Mum, looking around at Dad, who nodded and picked at his tie. He still looked like he was trying to hold back some kind of enormous joke. While Charlie squealed for joy and tried on her helmet, Mum looked at me. "We know you're not into horses, sweetheart, so I thought you would probably appreciate something to wear."

"Well, that's a no-brainer," said Josh. "All she ever goes on about is what she wears."

"Leave me alone for one night, can't you?" I said to him. "It's my birthday. Stop picking on me."

"It's not your birthday, really," he said. "And isn't the whole reason we're having this dinner tonight instead of yesterday on your actual birthday because you had to go on some stupid 'spa' trip with your barbie doll girlfriends all day?"

"Well, you can hardly talk," I spat back. "Look what you're wearing. Honestly—a flannel shirt? You can get those from the supermarket for nine bucks. You're embarrassing."

"Coco! Josh!" said Mum. "Stop it please." She looked

angry. "I am really sick of you picking on her, Josh."

Josh looked like a turtle pulling his head into his shell, so I gave him a smirk from across the table which was supposed to say *ha ha, I won*, but I didn't hide it well enough.

"Don't, Coco." Mum turned around to me. "He might be being mean to you, but sometimes you deserve it. A little bit less obsession with clothes and your looks might be a good thing, young lady."

She stood up and started gathering plates, still looking at me. "You probably do need to learn that what you look like on the outside is not nearly as important as who you are on the inside."

I pursed my lips, but made a tiny sorry face at her and rolled my eyes when she turned away.

"Now, I'm going to get the cake. And when I come back I want you two to have apologised to each other." She walked out to the kitchen.

"Sorry," Josh muttered at me with a grimace on his face.

"Sorry," I squeaked, sticking my tongue out at him. He stuck his back out at me and then Charlie made a face at us as well and we all started to giggle uncontrollably. "You look like a chicken when you do that," I said to her, gasping for air.

"Buck buck buck," she said, making the face and setting me off again.

Mum came back to the table with an enormous tiramisu on a cake plate. "Alright, if you've stopped being chickens, let's have some cake," she said. She was just about to put it down in front of Charlie and me when my dad spoke.

"Hold on, Deborah," he said.

We all turned and looked at him.

"I think before we have the cake, I need to tell you all something. We can eat the tiramisu afterwards to help celebrate it." Now he was grinning from ear to ear.

I raised an eyebrow at Charlie as if to say, *did you know about this? What's going on?* She shrugged back at me. *No idea.*

Mum put the tiramisu down and went back to her seat. "What are you going to tell us?" she said. "You look like it's very important."

"Oh, it is," he said, still grinning. "You'll guess in a second. You know how the other night you and I were looking at that real estate website?" he said to Mum.

"Ye-e-es," she said, looking expectant and pleased but wary at the same time.

"Well, I have an announcement to make," he said. He looked around at our wide-eyed faces.

"We're all going to have a big life change. I've bought a farm for us and we're going to move from the city to the country. We'll be on our new property by the beginning of next term."

The first noise I heard was a massive whoop out of Josh's mouth. Mum's eyes were popping out of her head, but the smile on her face said that she was happy and she expected it all along. Charlie was screaming for joy and yelling, "I'm going to have a pony, I'm going to have a pony." Dad was laughing, looking around and enjoying the surprise and the delight and the reactions from them all.

But there was no reaction from me. At least, not at first. I was frozen to my chair, my new skinny jeans still on my lap and the half-scrunched wrapping paper in one hand.

Then I felt a white-hot flame of rage and fear burst up from my feet to my mouth. I jumped to my feet, pushed my chair behind me, screamed at the top of my lungs and ran, as fast as I could, out of the dining room and all the way up two staircases, crying and sobbing as I went. At the top of the stairs, just before storming into my room and slamming the door behind me, I turned around and yelled at them all.

"I hope you're happy. You've completely ruined my birthday. And my life."

# CHAPTER 6

Normally we're not allowed to slam doors—it's another one of Mum's toilet cleaning offences. (If you break a rule, she doesn't yell. She just gets the toilet brush and holds it out to you. We have a lot of toilets and most of them are very clean.)

But there are some times in your life where a door slam is completely and utterly necessary. This was one of them.

I threw myself on my bed gasping for breath. My hands were shaking. I was so angry and upset that I was practically hyperventilating.

This was unbelievable. Was my dad crazy? How does someone who carries a briefcase, wears a tie and catches the bus to work at a bank every day just suddenly announce, out of nowhere, that a whole family is going to move? From the city to a farm? And in the next six weeks?

I couldn't help it. I actually started talking out loud, even though there was no one else in the room.

"It's not fair! Not not not not fair!"

My mind was whizzing with protests. *He's not the*

*only one in this family. I have rights too. And I don't want to go anywhere. I love this house and I love the beach. And what about school? He wants to drag me away from my life and plonk me on a farm! I don't do farms. They smell, they're muddy and there's nothing to do.*

I rolled over and thumped my fists on my bed. Did Dad expect me to cheer like Charlie and Josh? I mean, they love that stuff. Charlie could spend her whole day on a horse. Josh would give anything to drive a tractor around. They didn't care about mud and dirt and icky things.

Tears were prickling out of my eyes so I threw my hand over the side of my bed and scrabbled around for a box of tissues. I blew my nose snottily and dabbed at my face, trying not to wreck my mascara.

I turned to the teddy sitting on my bed. He was white with gold flecks in his fur and his name was Ruffles. I got him for my fifth birthday and for some reason he had the sort of face that just looked like he was listening to me. I snuggled right up to his nose and looked him in the eyes. He stared back like he understood.

"Yesterday it was like it was all beginning. And today it's all ending. My future, according to Dad, is gumboots and mud. I mean, a farm? For real? And I won't get to see my friends except for holidays and..."

I sat up suddenly, my eyes opened wide. Friends? Forget friends. This was it for me. There was no way that I could tell Saffron, Tiger and the other girls in the group about Dad's ridiculous plans. I would be dropped so quickly and so hard that you'd be able to hear the sound of my bum hitting the floorboards from the other side of

Sydney.

I started sniffling again. This was even more of a disaster. I'd be a country bumpkin for the rest of my life and no cool, beautiful people would ever want to talk to me again and my skin would get rough and I would never be able to go shopping for trendy stuff because there are no decent shops in the country, not that it would matter because no one who was any good lived on a farm anyway.

"I might as well move to the moon," I sniffed to Ruffles. "And the only friend I'll have left will be Sam because once I get the flick they'll just move on to the next person."

The next person! I hadn't even thought of that. There would be at least twenty more girls clawing to take my place, all of whom would be super-happy to see me go. All the hard work that I'd done to get into the group would have been pointless.

"I am so angry," I said firmly to Ruffles, holding his arms so tight that he probably would have squeaked if he'd been alive. "If this is true, and Dad isn't just playing a joke, I don't know if I will ever get over it. I am going to hate living on a farm. I am going to hate all the ugly country people."

I turned over, looked at my ceiling, narrowed my eyes and pulled my teddy bear in front of my face.

"And, Ruffles," I said, "I am probably, no, I'm definitely, going to hate my dad forever."

I needed to have another cry. A serious cry. Forget about the mascara—my face was over for the day. After about ten minutes of wet and snot I noticed that my tears were starting to make stains on my purple satin pillow case so I sat up, gulping and sobbing, and sat limply on the side of my bed. My hair was thrown all over my head but for once I totally didn't care.

After a few minutes I heard noises on the stairs and then there was a tap at my door and Charlie stuck her head around.

"Are you okay?" she said, coming to sit on the bed. She put her arm around me.

"What do you think?" I said bitterly. "I mean, moving to a farm? Is Dad for real? Is he crazy? He's a merchant banker, for Pete's sake."

"I think he really is going to do it," said Charlie. "I mean, it is kind of crazy, but I think it will be okay."

I groaned and threw myself back onto the bed, face down.

"I'm going to hate it!" I said, muffled by the cushions. It sounded more like Ibgodahadet. I put my head up again for air. "There's just no way I can be happy on a farm."

Charlie bumped down on the bed next to me. Our chins were nearly touching.

"I know," she said. "I know you'll hate it. I know you're going to be miserable." She propped herself up on her elbows. "But at least you can be miserable with me there."

I stuck my tongue out at her and tried not to smile. "Sometimes I just do not believe that we are twins. Who are you, strange person? Why am I the only one of my kind in this family?"

Charlie flopped over on her back and stuck her legs

up in the air. Her big toe on her left foot was poking through her sock as usual. She picked at her toenail.

"They want you to come downstairs. We're going to talk about it. Dad's got pictures from the internet up and everything." She flicked the bit of toenail away on to my floor and I shuddered involuntarily.

"Gross, Charlie, don't do that. Pick your toenails in your own room." I said.

"Well, I can't, because you're in here and I want to be with you. If you want to get me out of your room you'll have to come with me," she said, rolling her head around so she could see my disgusted face.

"Oh, alright." I sat up. "But I'm not going to be happy. This whole farm thing is completely ridiculous. Give Dad a week. As soon as he sees sense, he'll be back to normal."

I stood up and checked my mascara in the mirror. Streaks. Big ones. "Let me just fix this and then I'll come."

I grabbed a cotton ball and wiped my face, reapplied my eye liner and straightened up my mashed hairdo.

"Here," said Charlie, holding out something small. "Your bindi fell off."

I peeled it off her finger and pressed it firmly back on my forehead. If I had to go and talk about insane life changes with my crazy dad, I would do it with as much style as possible.

# CHAPTER 7

Taking a deep breath I followed Charlie down the stairs. As we went into the lounge room I held up my chin slightly, tightened my mouth and walked with exaggerated model-like steps over to the sofa. Looking from left to right I surveyed the room and sat with a flourish, my back straight and my head high.

"Oh good, Coco," said Dad, putting his head up from the laptop on the coffee table. "You've come back. I was just about to show everyone the photographs of the farm on the website."

Mum smiled at me, an encouraging sort of smile. "It really looks great, Coco," she said. "You okay?"

This was unbelievable. Did they have no idea that when I ran out of the dining room screaming it was because I was definitely not okay? I don't think Dad had even really noticed that I had been gone for half an hour or more.

I blinked at Mum a few times with a stern face, hoping that she would get the message that I was angry. I didn't want to talk. I thought I'd just burst out crying which wouldn't be dignified or stylish at all.

She opened her mouth to speak but just at that point Dad started to talk.

"So here it is," he said, adjusting the screen so that we could all see.

Josh and Charlie were kneeling by the coffee table sticking their heads in close trying to see the photograph of a big green field. They looked like 10 year-olds. I stayed on my sofa, refusing to be keen.

"It's a hundred acres, with a stream running right through. It backs on to national forest and it has quite a few different paddocks, and an olive grove and a piggery," said Dad. He had a huge smile on his face, and I've never heard his voice so excited. He was whipping through the photographs like he couldn't show them fast enough.

"Oh, it's so beautiful," said Mum. "Just look at all that land — and the view!"

"Are we going to get pigs?" asked Charlie. "I think they're so cute."

"I don't know yet," said Dad. "We will just have to take it slowly and see what we can do. There are no pigs in the shed at the moment."

*Pigs?* I thought to myself. My mouth tightened. *I'm never going in a pig shed. You can forget that!*

"So where exactly is it?" said Josh. "What's the nearest town?"

Dad fiddled around for a minute and brought up a map on the screen. "Here we are in Sydney." He pointed to a large yellow spot. Then he moved his finger down ten centimetres.

"This is it here, approximately," he said. "It's about

two hours south, just in from the coast. I guess the nearest town is probably Kangaroo Valley.

*Kangaroo Valley?* I thought to myself. My neck felt tight. *That's not even a town. It's a postcard caption.*

We visited Kangaroo Valley on our last family holiday. Well, I say visited, but I mean 'stopped in'. It's the tiniest little pit stop I've ever been through. If ever there was a town that was blink-and-you-miss-it, it's Kangaroo Valley. It had a bakery. And a shop selling rocking horses. And I think that was it. Oh, wait, there was also a sign saying 'World's Best Pies'.

*As if. I don't even like pies. Could this be any worse?*

Oh yes, it could.

"But it's not in town," said Dad. "It's about 30 kilometres out. It's down a fire trail. And apparently if it rains a lot the road gets cut off sometimes."

"Awesome," said Josh.

"That's cool," said Charlie.

Mum put her hand on Dad's and held it like she was really pleased. No-one even looked at me.

*Out of town? Down a fire trail? And the road gets cut off?* My back got straighter and straighter. Could this be any worse at all?

Oh, yes. Oh, yes, it definitely could.

"Dad, where's the house?" asked Charlie. "Is that the end of the photos? They don't have any pictures of the house."

Dad's eyes lit up. He looked like a little boy about to open a long-awaited Christmas present.

"Well, this is the best bit. There is no house!"

We looked at him blankly.

"We're going to build it ourselves!" he exulted, throwing his hands out wide as if he was inviting us all to the best party in the world.

"Oh my goodness!" said Charlie, but she was smiling.

"This is awesome!" yelled Josh.

"Oh, David," said Mum. "This is your dream, isn't it! You've always wanted to do this—and now you are!" She actually hugged him. They looked at each other with dewy eyes and then, *urrrgh*, they kissed on the lips. *Spare me, Mum and Dad. That's disgusting. Parents should not kiss.*

"I said there were no pigs in the shed. So we can clean it out and live there," Dad said, his words practically falling out of his mouth with excitement. I just about fell off my chair. But it didn't seem to stop him talking. "It has power and water and we can set up a camp kitchen. And the house shouldn't take too long to build if we all do it together. Maybe half a year?"

That was it. I'd had enough. Dad started burbling on about passive solar this and that, own vegie patch *blah blah, yada yada,* mud bricks, compost toilet, eco-friendly *ra ra ra,* completely self-sufficient. And from the looks of it, everyone else thought he wasn't crazy. He'd obviously infected them with some greenie-wildlife-warrior virus that I was (thankfully) immune to. Or he'd turned into some sort of magician/cult leader/crazy man and they'd all been brainwashed. There was no other explanation.

I had to say something. I had to put a stop to this insanity.

Rather than tears and yelling and protests, which obviously hadn't worked the first time, I decided to try to knock holes in his arguments.

"Dad," I said. "It sounds lovely." I stretched out the word laah-ve-ly as long as I could. "But really. I don't think this is going to work. You want us all to live in a pig shed," and here I shuddered for effect, "for six months while we all build a house out of mud. But the fact is, we..." and I gestured to Charlie, Josh and myself, "...need to go to school. We just won't have time to help build a house, however environmentally-friendly and wonderful and all that stuff it is. Plus, if it does rain and the road does get cut off, we'll have to miss days. And I know you think getting a good education is the best thing we can do to have a good start to our lives, right?"

I looked around with the warmest, friendliest expression on my face that I could muster. The image I wanted to send was of a girl who loved school so much that she couldn't bear to miss even an hour.

"So, even though it's a really great adventure," and here I put on a super-smiley face and made my voice sensible and comforting, "I just don't think it's practical. Maybe we should just go for a holiday to a farm. That would be fun."

"Come here, Coco," said Dad, still smiling. He patted the cushion of the sofa he was sitting on and made like he wanted to hug me. I cringed stiffly away.

"I have an even bigger surprise for all of you," he said. "How would it be to take a year off school? We can home-school while we get the farm set up and the house built. It'll be a huge education in heaps of ways. You guys can help build in the day time and then we'll do catch up school lessons at night. We won't have a TV or the internet for a while, so you won't have anything else to do."

I felt ill. My head was spinning and my heart was pounding. No TV? No internet? Home school? Was my dad insane? What had gotten into him? This couldn't be real. Surely I wasn't hearing this? No one was even listening! Dad had gone nuts and everyone else thought it was wonderful. What had happened to my family? How had normal Eastern Suburbs people suddenly been transformed into a bunch of crazy, mud-loving tree-huggers?

My happy face dissolved into a pout. I stood up, wobbling slightly on my legs which felt like jelly, opened my mouth and screamed like a baby.

*Waaaaaaah.*

Then I ran out of the room, still screaming, thundered up the stairs and slammed my door—again—behind me.

If they were going to go crazy, I could too.

# CHAPTER 8

When Mum and Dad finally came up to my room to try to cheer me up (ha!) I was face down again on the bed. This time I didn't care about the mascara streaks on the pillows. Black marks on purple satin are tiny problems when the rest of your life is ruined.

They tapped on the door and pushed it open tentatively.

"Coco?" said Mum. "Can we come in?"

I stayed with my face down and didn't even answer. There didn't seem to be much point. They were going to do what they were going to do anyway, and nothing I said was going to make any difference.

Mum took silence to be agreement and tiptoed in like she was trying to save my feelings or my dignity or something. Dad followed her, looking around in surprise. I didn't think he'd been up here since I was about eight. He sat awkwardly on my beanbag with his knees up to his ears and fingered a velvet cushion as though he had never seen one before.

I flipped over onto my back, but I kept my eyes firmly fixed on the ceiling.

"Coco, sweetie," said Mum, sitting down on my bed beside me and trying to put her arm around me. "I know this is all a big shock, but why aren't you at least trying to see the positives?"

I shrugged off her hand and moved my eyes to the corner of the room.

"Oh come on honey," she said. "You have to at least talk about it. Look, we're here together. We want to talk about it with you."

I steeled my face and sat up, turning my back to Dad and completely ignoring him.

"Did you know about this?" I asked her accusingly. "How can you just sit there and let Dad pull a huge life change onto us all with no warning at all? And then just agree to it. I mean, who knew any of this?"

"Well, it's not quite true that there was no warning at all," said Mum. She shifted back and looked at me oddly. "I mean, Dad's been talking about being unhappy in his job for at least a year now and the bank has been cutting staff for a year and a half. Surely you knew that? And we went for that holiday down the coast and we were looking in real estate windows... you remember that, right?"

All I remembered was a boring trip away last year staying in a daggy cabin on a smelly farm, with no shopping malls worth visiting, patchy mobile service, bad cafe food and Josh being mean to me. Oh, and the world's best pies. *Yeah, right.*

"This whole thing came from that?" I said. "But that was like, months ago. And you always look in real estate windows all the time, wherever we go. I thought that was just one of the weird things parents do."

Mum looked at me, slightly confused. "Yes, but normally when people look in real estate windows it means they just might be looking for real estate, right? Anyway, you knew that lots of people from Dad's firm were being offered redundancies starting about six weeks ago, didn't you? If Dad didn't lose his job now, he almost certainly would have in the future. He took the redundancy this week." Now she looked frustrated. "Surely we told you this? I know we told you this. Weren't you listening?"

I shrugged my shoulders. "I guess. I don't really pay much attention to that stuff. But anyway, this is different. I didn't think you'd do anything like this. It's another whole step to go and buy a farm and move to the country and build a house and home school. It's going to be terrible for us all!"

Dad spoke up. He was still squashed into my beanbag. "Actually, Coco, I think it's going to be amazing for us all." He fought his way out of a pile of cushions and stood up.

"This is an opportunity for our family to be together in a way that we'll never have again," he said. "You guys are all growing up. And I've been working way too many hours for too long."

His face got all excited and his hands started whirling around. "I just think we need to spend time with each other before life takes over and we start to head off in separate directions."

*Hmmmph!* I thought to myself, pursing my lips. *You're just taking me in your direction and I don't want to go.* But

Dad didn't seem to notice my face. He just kept on talking.

"This is something we can all do together as a family so that we spend more time together. I read a book this year that made me really think about stuff, and I think we need to do something meaningful together. Basically we need some adventure in our lives."

His face was all lit up, like a little boy who had just been given a new puppy.

"I've been wanting to do this for years, but I never talked about it because I never thought it could happen. And then I guess I wanted to surprise you all. It seemed like it would make it even more of an adventure."

I raised my eyebrows. "What about Mum? It seems a bit mean to spring something like this on her out of the blue."

"I'll admit he took me by surprise," Mum said. She moved over to sit at my dressing table. "But I have to say I'm not really shocked. It's been a little secret dream of mine too. Living cooped up in the city has never been my favourite thing."

Dad made a move to sit next to me. He was trying to make amends, but I wasn't about to let him.

"Come on, Coco," he said, putting an arm around me. "It's not going to be that bad. Surely you can get over the shock and think positively. There must be something that gets your imagination excited about all of this."

I pulled away and played with the tassel of the purple cushion on my lap. I couldn't talk. I just felt like I was going to cry. I had a black pit in my stomach and a burning volcano in my head.

"Isn't there anything you like at all?" he said again.

"No," I sputtered. "I can honestly say that there is nothing I like about this plan. Nothing at all. I can't believe you're doing this to me. It just all feels like I'm in a bad dream."

I was pretending to look away, trying to keep the tears in, but I saw Mum and Dad exchange a look. Mum shrugged her shoulders and Dad made a face. He nodded at Mum as if to say, 'go on, tell her.'

"Look," said Mum. She had her 'lets-all-calm-down' voice on. When she uses it, it sounds like she's talking to little kids. I think it used to work on Charlie and me when we were five, but it hasn't since then.

"Coco. Sweetie. Why don't you agree to give it a year? If you really, really hate being on the farm after twelve months, we can work out something. Maybe you can come back to Sydney for school and be a boarder. We don't want you to be unhappy, really truly. That's not what this is about. But we think it would be good to give the whole thing a try. Just for a year."

I turned over on the bed in a thump and glared fiercely at the ceiling. The top of my purple canopy mosquito net quivered from the jolt. I knew I was beaten. Screaming and fighting any more was never going to change it. I had to give in. But I wasn't going to give in completely. I still had some weapons up my sleeve.

"All right," I said, between clenched teeth. "I will give it a year. But I can tell you this. I'm not going to be happy. I'm not going to like it. And I'm definitely coming back to Sydney as soon as the year is over."

Mum and Dad raised their eyebrows at each other.

"That's my girl," said Dad, and he reached out to stroke my head.

I rolled out of his reach, stuck my head up and looked at him full in the face.

"Stop it, Dad. I'm only doing this because I have no choice. Okay, sure, I'll do the year. I'll stick it out. But just so you know how angry I am, I'm not going to talk to you for the next twelve months."

"Coco!" said Mum. "Don't be rude to your father!" Her face was red and her eyes were flashing.

"No, Deborah," said Dad, "it's okay. If she can't talk to me yet, that's fine." He looked surprisingly calm and unworried. "It was a shock. She probably needs some time to be on her own now."

He stood up and went to usher Mum out of the door. "Come on, let's go downstairs. She'll come down when she's ready."

*Much you know*, I thought furiously. *I'll never be ready.* But I went down anyway, stomping my feet and tossing my hair and making sure that they knew I was still cross. There was birthday cake down there and I wasn't going to miss out on my once a year tiramisu just because my dad had turned into the world's biggest nutcase.

# CHAPTER 9

On the bus to school the next day, Samantha was shocked and then firm.

"You definitely can't tell," she said, shaking her head. "Not even one word. If Saffron and Tiger found out about any of it, you'd be dropped straight away. And if you're coming back in a year, like your mum said you can, it's best just to keep it quiet."

"I know," I said, half groaning, "but how can I explain a whole year away? I can't say we're going overseas. For a start, I'm a hopeless liar and when I come back they'll know I haven't been in France or wherever for a year because all I can say is 'bonjour' in a really bad accent."

"I've got an idea," said Sam, sitting up in her seat and turning towards me. "You said that Charlie got a horse-riding helmet for her birthday. On a farm you're probably going to learn to ride, right? And you will be changing schools, kind of, yeah?"

"Yes..." I said, curious.

"Well, why don't we say that you're going to some sort of exclusive equestrian boarding school in the country—I don't know—in another state even, with

Charlie for a year?" she said. "You can tell everyone, which is kind of true, that your parents really want you to learn to ride well. And you can make it up that the school is so exclusive and strict and stuff that boarders aren't allowed to have phones or use Skype or email or anything. So that way you won't get anyone visiting you or finding out what's actually going on."

My eyes widened and the anxious pain in my neck I'd been carrying around since slamming my door the night before seemed to slide down my back and into the bus upholstery.

"That might work you know," I said slowly. "It's not too much of a lie that it's completely wrong. It's just kind of bending the truth. But it might work out so that I finish up not being too much of a loser."

I smiled at Samantha and put on the silly voice that we use when we say serious things. It's kind of a cross between an American and a Scottish accent. "You're a lifesaver and a true friend. Don't ever change!"

She grinned and shook her hand up near her face, like she was trying to cool down. "I'm good, huh?" she said in her matching silly accent. "Oh yes, sometimes I can't believe how good I am. I'm sneaky and crafty! Just call me 'the manager'."

I pretended to punch her in the arm and she shrank back in mock horror. "Watch out, you'll get my uniform grubby, you muddy little farm animal!"

I rolled my eyes and looked at my fingers, examining my manicure. "Ha! You say that like it's funny. Can you imagine? Last night Dad was saying things like we'll live in a pig shed." I shuddered. So did Sam. "And we'll be building a house! My nails are going to be shot after the first week!"

"Ssh," warned Sam, looking around as if she was expecting to see Tiger Lily in the next seat. "If you want to keep it a secret, you really can't talk about it. From now until you go, you're sticking to the story. You're going off to learn dressage and show jumping and horsey stuff. And you're coming back to school at the end of the year. No mud, no building and especially no pig sheds."

The bus was pulling up to school and as we got off, I made a face and pretended to zip my mouth shut and throw away the key. Sam made a movement like she was catching it and putting it in her pocket.

"Your secret is safe with me," she said dramatically and pushed me along. "Now go. Be popular and beautiful. And quiet!"

It was tricky. I actually have always been a person who likes to talk a lot. If my head is full of thoughts, I tend to blurt them out regardless of where I am or who's listening. It was something I wanted to change about myself because it's kind of uncool. Silent, aloof girls who have a single witty comment to throw in at exactly the right place seem way more attractive.

So far I'd worked really hard to hold my tongue around Saffron, Tiger and the others. I wanted them to see me as cool, intelligent and unconcerned. But now I really did have to keep my mouth shut. This was a secret that I had to keep. My reputation and my entire social future depended on it.

"So, everyone's coming to Westfield this afternoon?" Saffron said at recess, a piece of delicately wrapped sushi heading from her ultra-chic lunch box towards her lightly glossed mouth. She opened her mouth slightly and just kind of absorbed the sushi, hardly moving her jaw to chew. I was mesmerised by the way she ate. No, actually, that's not entirely true. I was mesmerised by the way she did everything. I couldn't get over how one person could be so perfect.

"Monday afternoon is shopping time," Tiger Lily said, with a sideways glance to me, as if to explain. I nodded furiously so I could show that yes, I knew and that yes, I was free and wanted to go, and then I realised that I was looking a bit too keen so I pulled back on the nodding and said, in what I thought was a cool, unconcerned sort of voice, "Oh, yeah, that's right. Um, yep, I can come."

"Nail polish!" said Lise, suddenly, holding up her hand to the light. She had a worried expression on her face and Isabella came to her rescue.

"I see what you mean. Wow, Lise. What is with your nails? Didn't you get another bottle last time we went?" she asked.

Lise shook her head furiously. "Forgot!" she said mournfully. Her big blue puppy dog eyes seemed so upset that I wanted to help her feel better.

"Oh, I need to get some too," I said looking around at the group, "so that's good. We can get it at the same place. It's so annoying that we can't wear anything at school but pink."

There was a short silence. Lise looked at Isabella and Saffron glanced sideways at Tiger who began an eye roll before Saffron put her hand on her arm like a warning.

"No, it's okay," she said calmly tossing her ponytail.

"She's still learning."

My heart sank. Obviously I had made a huge error but I had no idea what it was. If that wasn't bad enough, I started to feel my face beginning to turn pink. A ray of shame crawled up my spine. *Go away, go away, go away,* I thought to myself, trying to get control of my face.

Saffron leant in to me.

"Coco, we don't wear pink nail polish," she said, very seriously. She was saying it kindly, as though she really wanted to help me. "Everyone else does that. But we're not like everyone else. As you know." She said it meaningfully.

I nodded, grateful for her time.

"Oh, I know, I mean..." I stumbled. "I just— I didn't..."

"It's okay," she said. Her face was reassuring, and then suddenly flinty. "Just don't say it again."

I hardly trusted what might come out of my mouth, so I kept it closed and nodded quickly again. Lise was still holding her hand up, examining her nails and without even thinking I shot a quick glance towards her fingertips. If her nail polish wasn't pink, then what was it? Tiger Lily, impatient as always, saw my look and decided to inform me.

"It's greige," she said, looking up into the sky and away from me. "And before you have to ask what greige is, it's grey and beige. You have to read magazines to keep up with things, you know."

"Oh, right, I know," I said. My head was still going on a furious nod. I felt like a little Happy Meal toy. *Boing boing boing.*

Saffron leaned over to me again.

"I think your nails would look great in greige," she said. "Show me."

I held out my hand and she had a look at my fingers.

"Wow, great shape and great length," she said. "For nails that you've obviously done yourself, they're pretty good. Imagine what they'll look like when you get a proper manicure!" She looked up at me. "I presume you'll be getting one soon, right?"

My mouth felt like it was about to blabber and stumble again but I managed to get control. "Yeah, of course. This is just my emergency polish."

I could see Tiger Lily take a breath to speak again and was just about to duck my head when, like a sudden cool breeze on a boiling hot day, the bell went and I was saved.

I walked to maths telling myself to pull it together.

"Don't be such a loser, Coco. Get hold of yourself. You can do this."

I took some breaths and calmed down, opened my books and then spent the next fifty minutes pretending to listen to fractions and decimals while actually I was thinking about something way more important — the lies I was going to tell and the stories I was going to spin about why I was going away.

# CHAPTER 10

Samantha and I waited a few more days before I spilled the beans.

First we needed to do our research. I couldn't just invent an equestrian boarding school in another state one morning and expect everyone to believe me. I could be found out in a second if someone Googled it on their phone under their desks in history.

We couldn't believe it when we discovered Lamerton Grammar for Girls. Not only was it interstate, horse crazy and a boarding school, it also had a rural (read: in the middle of nowhere) campus where, according to the website, Year Eight girls went to grow their own food, live without technology, learn to run a farm and excel at horsemanship. Apparently all of this was so that they would 'build character'.

It sounded completely revolting.

"Honestly, like, who needs character?" said Sam. She grimaced and then checked the mirror. "I really shouldn't do that. It's going to make lines on my face," she said, smoothing out her cheek. "Look, can you see a wrinkle starting? Seriously, though. Give a girl a manicure, a good haircut and some bronzer and she's good to go. No character required."

"I know, right? In real life—you know, out in the real world—it's probably more useful to have a good wardrobe than to have character," I said. "So glad I'm not going to that school. Maybe there actually *is* something worse than going to live on a pig farm with my family."

I laughed, but Sam didn't get the joke. She raised her eyebrows. "No. There's not. And let me tell you, unless you can convince Tiger Lily that you're telling the truth about this Lamerton Grammar thing, you are going to be dropped into a big pile of pig poo. There won't be any 'character' that will be able to rescue you. You'd better make this thing stick."

"I wish there was a character who was going to rescue me," I said, groaning. "Do you realise that we're probably going to be gone before I even get to meet Darcy?"

"That's such bad timing," said Sam. "Why did he have to go skiing for so long? Now you'll have to wait a whole year."

"Which is like, forever, when you think you've found the boy of your dreams," I said sadly. "Seriously, he is gorgeous. You have no idea."

"There probably won't be any decent boys near you at all," said Sam. "And even if there are you won't get to meet any if you're stuck on the farm all day."

"I know, right?" I agreed. "And anyway—farm boys? Eew."

"Look, if by some miraculous chance I ever get to meet Darcy, I promise I'll tell him about you and what he's missing," said Sam. "You never know. Maybe you two are just meant to be."

"You're such a great friend," I said. "You look out for me! Are you going to be okay when I'm gone? I'm worried you'll be left alone with no friends."

She gave me a joking, sceptical look. "Are you serious? Don't worry about me. Worry about yourself. You've got to nail this story. Both of our futures depend on it."

So I learned to lie. I practiced in front of the mirror a few times to build my confidence and then fielded mock questions helpfully prepared by Samantha.

"Why can't you just do horse riding here like everyone else?" she demanded to know, pretending to be Tiger Lily and adding an eye roll for dramatic flair.

"Well, my parents really like the idea of us doing something away from home," I said glibly. "They're all into 'building character' and anyway, my mum went there for a while when she was young, so it's kind of like home away from home."

And so my story began.

I told the girls at lunch on Friday and spent a nervous weekend waiting for a message on my phone that said, "You're lying, you loser, we know everything and you're dropped!" but it never came. On Monday when the topic came up again, it seemed like I was safe. No one suspected a thing and I wanted to keep it that way.

At home, it seemed like Dad was on some kind of super-speed drug because everything was happening uber-fast.

"I've got it set for us to move on to the farm first week of the holidays," he told us at dinner. "So you can say all your goodbyes to friends in the next three weeks."

"Oh wow, that's so soon," said Charlie, enthusiastic. "I can't wait."

I sniffed haughtily and looked away.

I had been true to my promise and had managed not to talk directly to Dad for at least a fortnight. A couple of times in the first few days I nearly forgot and asked him to pass the salt at dinner but at the last second I managed to make it seem like I was actually talking to Josh.

Once he started giving us instructions about packing though, I nearly lost the plot. I had to literally bite my lips so that I didn't let out any words.

"So, you guys can take a suitcase each," he said. "Pack everything else into boxes so we can put it all into storage until the house is built."

I had to wait till I was in Charlie's room before I could start yelling about it.

"One suitcase? Is that all? Does he expect me to live with only one suitcase worth of clothes?" I said. "What about all my other stuff? I'm not going to cope without my make up and shoes and pillows and all the rest of it for a whole year."

"He did say one suitcase each," Charlie said. "You make it sound like we all have to put our stuff in the same suitcase altogether. Seriously. Get the big suitcase. You'll be fine."

I did. I got the biggest suitcase I could find. It was the one Mum bought the year that we all went to the Gold Coast and she said she was sick of handling a million different little pieces of hand luggage on the plane, but even then I couldn't make it all fit in. And I was studiously ignoring Dad's instructions to leave behind my good clothes.

"Two pairs of jeans, a pair of joggers, a couple of old T-shirts and a jacket or two," he kept saying over and over to anyone who would listen. "That's all you're going to need. And we'll buy gumboots for everyone before we go. We'll need them for the mud."

Mum was on the bandwagon as well. "Honestly, girls, don't pack your nice clothes. I'm serious. Maybe just one top or something, but you won't get a chance to wear them and they'll probably just get ruined until we've got the house up."

*I don't care,* I thought to myself. *I'm not going to look like a complete dag for 12 whole months. I'll take my blue satin covered flats if I want to. And my white lacy shirt and my best leggings and my silver sandals and my vintage clutch and my…*

When Charlie saw my suitcase she laughed.

"Coco, you're crazy," she said. "I've got three pairs of jeans, jodhpurs, riding boots and my five worst T-shirts. Mum is going to freak when she sees all of yours."

But Mum was keeping her cool. It was a tense stand-off between her and me to see who would crack first. Every time I deliberately ignored Dad or spoke to someone else when I could have spoken to him I saw her face get tight. I could see she wanted to yell at me but she and Dad obviously had some kind of pact going on—a kind of 'lets see how long she can go on with this for' agreement.

When she came into my room and saw my suitcase bulging at the sides she said nothing except, "there won't be any electricity for your hair dryer, honey," and then walked away.

The hairdryer stayed in the suitcase. And I added in my straightening iron for good measure. I needed to stay angry. It was either that or burst out crying. When Mum started pulling all the pictures off the walls and packing them away in brown paper I had to go for a walk and blink back my tears. When the removalists came to take away the furniture I had to run upstairs to hide the large gulpy sobs I could feel coming up from my stomach. My life was getting dismantled in a crazy tornado of activity and no one cared that I was sad.

*I'll be back in a year, I'll be back in a year.* I kept the thought running grimly through my head as we packed and prepared and as Dad ran around with a grin that got bigger and bigger all over his face. *I'll be back in a year,* I thought. *I've just got to make sure no one finds out where I've gone.*

On the last day of term, the girls took me out after school for a final farewell drink.

"Honestly," said Tiger Lily. "Parents. Why do they have to do these stupid things?" She sipped her drink (diet, of course) and rolled her eyes.

Lise opened hers wide with awe and wonder. "Horses!"

Isabella started a story about how a girl who she knew who went to one of these kinds of schools, you know, with a campus in the middle of the bush, and she was really, really good at riding and just was amazing with horses and everything, well, she loved it, just loved it, but she lived just like a nun—didn't see a boy for a whole year, can you imagine?

When she'd finally finished, Saffron just smiled at me.

"It's a shame. We've got quite used to you, Coco."

My stomach got nervous. That didn't sound good. Was this it? Were they going to dump me anyway? I tried to keep a neutral expression on my face but worry was escaping from the corners of my eyebrows.

"We've decided we'll ask someone else to be our number five while you're away," she said. "But it'll only be temporary. Once your year is up, we want you back here with us."

My eyebrows relaxed and I let out a quiet breath, trying not to look too relieved.

"Oh, of course, I mean, I'd expected you'd find someone else..." I said, trying not to sound like a puppy licking its mother's face. I was aiming to be casual. "So, um, do you know who . .?"

"You'll probably be happy," said Saffron. She smoothed down her hair and adjusted her skirt. "We're asking your friend Samantha. She was second on our list anyway. We only didn't pick her because we thought she was a little bit too pushy, but we'll let her know it's just for the year and then you'll be back in the group instead."

My face broke out into a smile that I just couldn't hold back. Finally, in what had been the worst month of my life ever, something good was happening. This was going to kill two birds with one stone. Samantha wouldn't end up lonely and miserable because I had gone, and she could keep things good for me in the group so that I could come back with no issues. Even better, she'd meet Darcy! *She could talk to him about me*, I thought. *Keep him interested...*

Isabella leaned over the table towards me. "So, are you, like, serious about the no internet or phone thing?

Not even email? No iPods, nothing?" she said. "Couldn't you just sneak something in?"

I shook my head dramatically. "No. It's super-strict. They really make a big thing about it. They have random room searches and if you're caught with one they send you to solitary for a week."

"Seriously?" said Tiger Lily. "Solitary? In this day and age?" She looked cynical. "It's against your rights."

"I know. But that's what it is apparently. It's all based on some kind of ancient philosophy that 'builds character'." I made quote marks with my fingers and a silly face and the girls laughed.

"And I bet all the teachers are ugly too," said Tiger Lily.

"Holidays?" asked Lise, turning her puppy dog eyes on me. "Home?"

"Maybe I'll be able to get back," I said. "But not much. It's going to be weird. I don't really know. I'll have to see how it goes. But it's only for a year and then I'll be back, like normal."

"So, here's to a crazy year!" said Saffron, holding up her glass. Everyone clinked and sipped and smiled.

"Don't worry about me," I said. "I'll be back before you know it. And mega-full of 'character'."

# CHAPTER II

Not even a week later I had turned into a Neanderthal.

My wildest imagination could not have prepared me for where our inner-city, café loving, beach babe family ended up. I could almost cope with the idea of looking like a grotty farmer for a year. I could nearly get my head around building a house. I was close to getting used to the idea of being two hours drive away from the city.

But reality, as they say, bites. Chomps, even. Chews, mashes and swallows. And then spits out the bones at the end.

The first clue that things might be even worse than I had expected came when we drove down what Dad optimistically called the 'driveway'.

"I'm getting out! Stop the car. Mum, tell Dad to stop the car. He's going to kill us," I was yelling about three minutes into our descent down the steepest hill on the slipperiest track I'd ever seen.

"It's okay, Coco. We have a four wheel drive. This is what these sorts of cars do," said Dad.

I ignored him, took a breath and kept screaming. "Stop the car! I'm going to die!"

Josh started to laugh at me. "Ha ha. Coco is a scaredy cat." But even his face went white as we bumped over about ten million big rocks in a row and I saw him start hanging on to the armrest.

Twenty whole minutes later the sandy track came out of the bush, turned past an olive grove and came to an end in a green field. Dad stopped the car so we piled out, stretching and rubbing our bruised and battered bottoms. Mum breathed in deeply and smiled. "Oh look at this, David. It's incredible. What a view."

I turned around to see. It was true. There was a view. And I'll admit it, it was pretty nice. Green paddocks, trees following a creek at the bottom of a small valley, and in the distance, black and white cows milling around some hay bales. Cute, if you like that kind of stuff. Which I do, but only on holidays and only in postcards.

Right now I had more pressing matters to think about.

"Mum—I need to go," I hissed, crossing my legs. That was another reason I had been screaming on the way down the driveway. Every time the car hit a rock I nearly wet my pants.

Mum stopped admiring the view and looked at me hopping up and down. "David, is there a toilet here?" she said, gesturing around the paddock.

"Uh, yeah? You think?" said Charlie, laughing. "There's nothing here."

"No. I meant in the shed. Does it work yet?" she said.

"There's a pit toilet near the shed. But I think it needs some treatment before it'll be ready for use," he said. "It won't take long though."

"Long? How long are we talking?" I wanted to yell, but

I wasn't talking to Dad so I had to hold it in. Meanwhile I was having trouble holding it in at the other end.

"Mum, I need to go," I said again, dancing now. "Seriously. Now."

She looked annoyed. "Okay then. Go."

I raised my eyebrows at her. "Um, where?"

"Where do you think?" she hissed back. "What, do you think I'm just going to magically produce a toilet out of thin air? Find somewhere."

I gaped at her. "What?"

"You're a big girl," she said. "Cope. Off you go."

I could feel tears starting to prickle but I blinked them back. "Fine," I said stiffly, and headed off to a line of bushes and trees down at the bottom of the paddock, my chin held as high I could push it. The plan was to look like I didn't care, but let me just say it's tricky to walk like you're dignified and cool when you're about to wee your pants, when you're trying not to step in cow pats and when you're trying to ignore your brother sputtering with laughter behind you.

I turned to yell back at him. "Just so you know, the pit toilet probably stinks. I wouldn't want to go there anyway!"

*This is so not funny, not fair, not funny, not fair,* I grouched to myself in my head. *Stupid, stupid, stupid. Who buys a stupid farm without a stupid toilet? Who has to go in the bushes? Stupid, not fair, dumb, stupid farm.*

I kept walking, trying to avoid stepping on sticks and cow poo, while keeping my legs practically crossed and trying to stick to the few bits of flat ground I could see. There were holes and hollows all over the paddock and

I didn't want to twist my ankle, especially not in white, lace-covered ballet flats, which I noticed were already getting reddish-brown around the edges, the colour of the dirt under the grass. *Great, now I'll have to clean my shoes too, I thought.*

When I finally reached the bushes I picked my way through the prickly bits until I couldn't see the others. *Finally,* I thought. *Some privacy.* I let out a big breath and blinked a few times to clear my eyes.

*That's a good spot over there,* I thought, seeing a little clear area behind a big dead branch lying on the ground. I started to undo the button of my jeans as I stepped forward, but the branch was bigger than I thought. *I'll have to jump. Careful...*

And that was when everything got much, much worse.

I took a small leap over the tree branch but by that time I had also undone my pants just enough so that my legs got confused about how long they were and tried to do more than was possible. Basically, it was a world-class trip up and I landed on my face on the other side of the log.

But that wasn't all.

As I landed I heard a splash. It was me, landing in a small stream of water.

But it wasn't just water. It was water mixed with dirt, which makes mud. I now had mud from my forehead to my knees. (My feet were still on the other side of the branch.) My hands were covered in dirt and as I got up, groaning, I instinctively went to brush them off on my jeans. It was only then that I discovered that the terrible smell that had just reached my nose was a cow pat which I had squashed in my fall and which was now spread out all over my thighs, on my jeans and now on my hands.

As bad as this was, I was determined to not let it get worse. I still needed to go. I knew that if I went back to my ridiculous family covered in mud, that would be bad enough. But I also knew that if I went back, having wet my pants as well, I would hear about it until my dying day.

*Yuck*, I said to myself. *Completely gross. But I can't deal with it now.* Wiping my hands on a little patch of grass, I continued on to the clear space I was going to use as a toilet. I squatted carefully over the grass and a few other green, slightly spiky plants I had never seen before and did, finally, what I so desperately needed to do.

*Aah, that feels better,* I thought. *Relief!* But I was nearly falling over, so I shifted myself slightly to adjust my balance. That, right there, was the thing I should not have done. As soon as I moved, a shooting, burning pain grabbed my bottom and spread down my leg and up my back.

I screamed.

Loudly.

I couldn't help it.

"My bum's on fire!" I said. "Help!"

If I had been dancing before, it was nothing to the jig I was doing now. The pain was stinging and burning and all I could think about was cooling it down somehow. Suddenly it came to me.

*I know! The water!*

Without even pulling up my jeans I shuffled over to

the mud puddle I'd fallen into before and sat, bottom first, in the water. I could almost hear the sizzle. It only helped slightly, it was true, but it was better than nothing and at least I wasn't screaming anymore.

About a minute later Mum and Charlie burst through the bushes.

"Coco! Are you okay?"

"We heard you yelling," said Charlie. "What's the matter?" And then she started to laugh.

"What's so funny?" I said, huffily. "I hurt my bottom, that's all. I'm okay."

"That's all?" said Charlie. "It doesn't look like that's all."

She had a point. I was sitting, wearing lace ballet flats and what was formerly a white T-shirt, in a stream with my pants down, covered in mud on my top half and smeared with smelly cow poo on my bottom half. She thought it was hilarious. But I didn't feel like laughing.

"Leave me alone." I stood up, ignoring my still slightly sore bottom, did up my jeans and walked carefully past Mum and Charlie, who was still standing there giggling.

"I'm fine."

"Coco, sweetie…" said Mum. But I ignored her and kept walking, out of the bushes and back up to the car. Behind me, Mum and Charlie were scrambling through the twigs and leaves.

*Hmmph*, I thought. *Could this day get any worse?*

Let me tell you: I've got to stop saying that. Because every time I do, something bad happens.

It wasn't until I was nearly back to Dad and Josh that I realised that there was something dripping down the back of my jeans on one side. It felt different from the water from the stream, so I put my hand on the back of my leg and nearly fell over when I pulled it back and looked at it.

My hand, previously covered in cow poo, was now totally red from blood. My blood! *Yes, this could definitely be worse*, I thought. *Don't cry, don't cry, don't cry.*

"Coco!" yelled Mum from behind me. "You're bleeding." Mothers are so good at stating the obvious. She ran up and pulled down my jeans, just like she would have if I was five years old. *Embarrassing much!* "Let me see!"

"Mum!" I started, squirming my head around, but I stopped talking when I saw a black blob stuck to my bottom. "Mu-u-um! What is that?" My tummy was clenching with fear. This was creepy. I nearly said, "Help, I'm going to die," but managed to stop myself in time.

I was frozen in fear, looking at this disgusting black thing attached to my bum, with blood pouring down my leg, when Charlie caught up to have a look. When she did, she started laughing all over again. This time she was rolling on the ground.

Fear disappeared. Now I was just mad at her. "What?" I snapped. "Why is this so funny?"

"Ha ha!" she gasped in giggles, clutching her stomach. "It's a leech!"

My eyes opened wide and I nearly lost my lunch. I felt sick to my stomach. A leech? An actual leech? On my bottom? *Eeew, yuck, ew, disgusting.* This was just too gross. But I was determined not to lose it and show them all I was a mess. So I curled up in a ball and pretended to be dignified and calm while Mum pulled the leech out and got some antiseptic cream and bandaids out of the car.

"Wow, Coco. You really stink," said Josh. "Waaay worse than a pit toilet." He held his nose. I stuck my tongue out at him, and then realised I had grit in my mouth. *Double icky gross.* I tried to spit it out without actually spitting but I ended up swallowing it instead.

It was at that point that I noticed my lace ballet flats were ripped. On both feet. *Disaster,* I thought. *My favourite shoes. Completely stuffed up by a stupid tree branch.* I sighed, and realised Mum was still dabbing blood off my leg.

"I think you got stung by a nettle," she said, taking a closer look at my bottom. *Thanks Mum. Great stuff. Check it all out.* "It looks like something's brushed up against you while you were going to the toilet."

"A nettle?" said Dad. "You've got to watch out for these things. There are some pretty vicious ones in the bush. Also, I probably should have reminded you—in fact, all of you guys—to be careful of snakes too. It's still the season for them. And there are some nasty Browns around in this area."

"Snakes?" I said. It was my first word to Dad in two months. "Snakes?"

And then I lost it. I cried. Sobbed, sniffled, snivelled, bawled, blubbed, howled, wept and wailed. And I didn't stop for the next two hours.

This was not supposed to be my life. I was not supposed to be stuck on the side of a mountain on a cow-pat filled paddock avoiding snakes and stingers and leeches, ripping my best shoes and going to the toilet in the bush. This was crazy-land. And for the next twelve months, there was no way out.

I was trapped.

# CHAPTER 12

Over the next few weeks I perfected the look that I called the Half Roll, where I opened my eyes as wide as I could, looked from side to side and did a slight downward roll of my eyeballs. It wasn't enough to get me into trouble with Mum who had a thing about rolling your eyes — it usually merited a toilet clean — but it was just enough for me to say, *Really? Are you kidding me? Is this the way it's going to be? I'm definitely better than this.*

I did the half roll when I saw the shed that was going to be our new house. *Seriously? This is disgusting.* Gravel on the floors, no proper walls — just corrugated iron — with a 'kitchen' that was nothing more than a portable stove and a camping fridge attached to a noisy little generator. I did the biggest half roll I could do when Dad set up my 'bedroom', which was basically a bed behind a shower curtain. I didn't even have enough room to put my suitcase out permanently. Every time I wanted to get dressed I had to hoick it on to my bed, choose my clothes and then put the thing away again.

The only thing I didn't make a half roll face for was the pit toilet. Yes, it smelt, but there was no mud, stinging nettles or leeches, and I guess I had to be grateful for something. I still made sure I checked for brown snakes (actually, for snakes of any colour — it's just that the brown ones can kill you) every time I went though. It would have been earth-shatteringly embarrassing to have ended up in hospital with a snake bite on my bottom.

Plus, I was trying to minimise the risk of dying in a place where I would probably have the most unfashionable funeral ever. Knowing Dad as I now did, it would be quite likely that he would bury me in a field somewhere and forget all about me. There would be no headstone with an elegant quote, no quietly sobbing people in black hats, no flowers and no yearly visits from my grief-stricken friends coming to lay memorial bottles of nail polish and rolls of sushi on my grave. No. If I was going to die I would have to wait at least twelve months until I got back to the city where I could do it properly.

Josh and Charlie took to the new life like they had been living it forever. They chopped firewood, helped Dad clear space for the house and explored the property with the kind of energy that you get when you put a brand new set of batteries in a set of slot cars. *Vrooooom.*

I was left with the run-down, mismatched dodgy batteries. The bargain bin, no-name ones with rust and grit on the ends. I hardly had enough energy to get out of bed.

"Come on, Coco," Charlie said to me every morning. "Let's go check out the creek/back paddock/olive grove," or whatever it was that day that was taking her interest. "What's the matter?"

"I don't really feel like it," I said. "I'll just stay here."

She looked at me concerned. "Are you sure? Do you want me to stay with you?" I shrugged and smiled at her, but it was a weak smile. "I'm okay here."

She stayed for three minutes but then her curiosity got the better of her and she was off. "I'll be back later. Promise."

"Okay," I said. "I'm just tired."

It was mostly true. Everything was an effort. With no electricity in the shed, I couldn't believe how much work it was to do even a simple thing like take a hot shower. You had to pump the water from the tank into a drum, build a fire underneath it to heat it up, wait three hours while it heated and then fill the camp shower with buckets of hot water. After that, if you got three minutes you were lucky.

Dad showed me how to do it in the first week. I gave him the half roll and even went to a full roll (out of sight of Mum of course) when he told me that he expected me to do it myself after that. But I couldn't imagine living without a shower at least once a day so I went through the whole rigmarole every day for a week before finally giving it up as a joke. There are limits to how much work I will do—even if it's to keep clean and maintain standards. I admitted defeat (but only to myself) and stuck to a simple face and hands routine with a bowl of warm water in the morning and a weekly shower and hair wash.

Life was ridiculous, difficult and grubby. I mean, this is the 21st century, right? As I told Charlie almost every day, people invented electricity and toasters and hairdryers for a reason — because life is better with them. But there was no convincing Dad. He was hopping around every morning like an excited bunny, talking to builders and making plans and marking and measuring and sticking rods in the ground and reading books and talking to Josh about farming and other stupidly boring things that made my head spin. At night he was holding his hands out in front of the fire, sighing and saying, "Oh, now this is living. This is how it's supposed to be." Half roll. *Please.* Charlie was talking about horses, and could she get one eventually, wearing muddy gumboots, jodhpurs and cowboy hats and sitting on fences like she'd never seen a city in her life. Even Mum, who I thought for sure would have cracked once she realised she'd either have to wash the clothes by hand or take huge loads to the laundromat a half hour's drive away (and that's after she'd made it up the driveway from hell) seemed to be enjoying it.

The days sorted themselves into a routine of food, chores, schoolwork, more chores, more food and more schoolwork. I did the half roll when Mum first pulled out books and pens and things. "Why even bother?" I muttered under my breath. "If we're going to live in Middle Earth, I don't think we need algebra. I'm sure that hobbits didn't learn biology."

As it turned out, there was a benefit to doing school at the farm. For one thing, it didn't take so long. I spent three hours doing stuff we took six to get through at school, so I was definitely saving time. The question was, though, for what? There was no TV, no internet, no electricity, nowhere to go and nothing to do. There was also no one to talk to.

Or so I thought.

When we first arrived I'd assumed we were living out here all alone, kind of like in the stories when someone gets marooned on an island in the middle of the ocean and there's no one around for miles and no way of contacting the mainland.

But apparently that wasn't so. Other people actually lived here in Budgong. By choice. And they liked it. Who knew?

We'd only been living in the shed for three weeks or so when I'd had yet another argument with Josh during my afternoon maths time (*Him*: No, stupid, you have to carry the one. Didn't they even teach you addition at school? How did I get such a dumb sister? *Me, lunging forward and pulling his hair:* Get out of my face you idiot!) and had been sent out of the shed by Mum to cool down.

I was wandering around the bottom of the paddock, kicking morosely at stumps of grass when I heard a low booming kind of noise. *A storm? Thunder?* I thought idly, but thunder is over quickly and this was getting louder. *Traffic? Oh. D'oh.* I smacked my forehead. There was a definite rhythm to it, a beating and drumming and then a kind of whooping and yelling. And then I could feel vibrations in the ground. *Earthquake? Just my luck.*

But then I saw them. Two enormous horses, one white and one brown, exploding out of the bush and racing across our paddock towards me. I'd never seen a horse gallop before and the two of them together looked ferocious. I thought horses were supposed to be nice, sweet things with ribbons in their manes and ridden by little girls, but let me tell you, that's a complete myth invented by the publishing industry who just want to sell pony stories. These horses looked crazy. One had its mouth open with scary teeth and the other was actually foaming and frothing.

I was confused for a second but then the panic hit.

*They're coming right for me*, I thought. I couldn't control the squeal that came out of my mouth and my legs took themselves, as fast as they could run, to hide me behind a tree stump. I squatted down, shivering with fright and hid my face in my hands.

Through my fingers I could see the horses pass me at what sounded like super-sonic speed but then I heard a yell and I saw the people riding wheel around and walk back towards me.

They stopped.

It was awkward.

There were two of them, on impressive looking horses, and only one of me, hiding behind a ridiculously tiny tree stump. Plus they'd just seen me squealing like a squashed guinea pig, my paws over my face. It wasn't what I'd call a good beginning.

"Hey, person behind the stump," said the boy. He was riding the brown horse, which turned out to be even bigger than it looked now that it was standing five metres from my face. It didn't stay still like the other one and kept dancing around slightly. The boy had to work hard to keep it under control. It was sweating too, which I could smell, and had big wet, foamy patches on its body under the saddle and down its back legs. I screwed up my nose. *Ew.*

"Hey, are you okay?" said the boy again, looking at me like he was concerned. I got up stiffly from my squat and tilted my chin at him, like there was nothing more normal than hiding behind a small wooden stump in a paddock in the middle of nowhere.

"What do you want?" I said, looking hard at him. He was about fifteen, I was guessing and wearing jeans, a blue flannelette shirt, a riding helmet and the most stupid looking pair of Cuban heeled cowboy boots you've ever seen. The sort of thing the extras wear in the old westerns that they play at midday in non-rating periods to fill up the TV schedules. Do people really wear these things for real? I looked up at the sky. *If this is where you've put me, take me now. I'm ready to die.*

The girl on the white horse stared at me. She was also in jeans, with (thankfully) normal riding boots, but her red t-shirt was clearly from the $4 table at K-mart and was, sadly, completely the wrong shape for her rather large chest.

"What are you doing here?" she said, and suddenly I could see the family likeness in them. Unfortunately for them, their family likeness wasn't a very good one. They both had sharp noses and the kind of blond hair that just looks dirty rather than beachy. They did have one good feature — their bright blue eyes. Eyes are crucial, I always think. But when everything else needs work, sometimes even perfect eyes are not enough.

*Brother and sister, definitely,* I thought. And Miss Wrong Shirt was probably just a bit younger than Mr Cuban Heels. Maybe thirteen or fourteen?

The girl spoke again from up high on her horse.

"Where are you from?"

"Yeah, who are you?" said her brother. He was still trying to make his horse stand still. It obviously didn't like him.

I suddenly felt small. Maybe it was the fact that both of them were perched metres above me on huge enormous animals that could have eaten me for breakfast. (Okay, I know horses are herbivores, but seriously, the teeth... ) Maybe it was the fact that I'd been caught out squealing and quaking with fear in the middle of a paddock. I don't know. But when I feel small, I get defensive.

"Who are you?" I snapped back. And then I got protective. "And what are you doing here?"

It was ironic, I know. I hated this paddock and all the rest of it—the creek, the shed, the property, the whole place, in fact—but at least it was *my* place to hate. Now these two style-deprived twits were trespassing and I was going to have something to say about it.

"Sorry?" said the girl. She looked quizzically at her brother. "We always ride here."

He nodded, looking straight at me. "Yup. This is where we ride. Since, like, for years." His face was earnest but I was angry.

"Are you kidding me?" I said. "You're on my land. I live here."

"Really? There's no house," said the boy, blinking. His voice was direct and his face seemed honest. And for some reason I didn't like that. At all. I'd been annoyed with him up until now. It was at this point that I started to actually hate him.

"There will be a house. We're building one." I said,

making my eyes hard. "Ever heard of real estate deals? That's where you buy and sell property. My family bought this property. That makes me the owner and you the person who doesn't get to ride here, since, like, for years."

I took a breath. "So you can take your cheap flannelette shirt and your sweaty horse and your whole Royal Easter Show thing," I waved my hand in the air towards him, "and you can ride away into the sunset. Bye bye."

The girl looked shocked and turned to her brother but he shrugged his shoulders at her. "Let's go," he said. "Anyway, look," he said, gesturing to his horse which was still dancing and snorting. "She's completely ready to go." As he turned his horse around he looked back at me and tried to smile. "Maybe see you later."

I tossed my head and put my hands on my hips and watched them ride away. It felt so good to have some power that I couldn't help it. I yelled after him.

"Oh, and your boots? Seriously. No-one actually wears those things except on Australiana-tourist 'throw another shrimp on the barbie' TV ads they make for Japanese visitors. They're a complete cliché."

I turned and trudged back up the paddock feeling smug and a bit pleased with myself. *Well done Coco*, I thought. *You've seen the last of them.*

I really should stop saying things like that.

Because they never turn out to be true.

# CHAPTER 13

It didn't take long before I proved myself wrong.

Again.

In fact, it was just the next day.

Mum was taking herself off to the Budgong Community Group 'to meet the neighbours'. "Want to come, Coco?" she said brightly as she changed into her cleanest pair of jeans and scraped the mud off her Blundstone boots which didn't look like they'd seen actual daylight through the muck that had been all over them for weeks. I think she was trying to build bridges, do some bonding. That sort of thing. "It might be fun."

I shook my head from my pillow where I was having yet another lie-down. "Not for me, thank you." For once I wasn't actually trying to be rude but Mum took offence.

"I was just asking. You don't have to take that tone, you know." *So much for the bonding.* "Fine. Stay home," she said. "I'll see you later."

I gave her a half roll. "Later, then," and flopped back onto my bed. *Neighbours,* I thought. *Ha. I'll bet they're all farmers over 85 who haven't been out of Budgong in 40 years. Mum's going to be bored as.*

Once again, I had to eat my words.

Mum came back, more sparkly and full of life than I've ever seen her.

"You won't believe how great these people are," she raved to Dad. "Beautiful people. And so welcoming. And we're invited to visit Ness who lives on the property over that way." She gestured out past the creek.

"Is she on her own?" asked Dad.

"I think so," said Mum. "I'm not quite sure, but from a couple of things she said I think she lost her husband young, and then she was with a guy who ended up being violent. He's gone now. But he wasn't the father of her kids."

"Kids?" said Charlie. Her eyes looked bright. "How old?"

"I'm not sure," she said. "From the sounds of it they're a bit younger than you guys. A boy and a girl. But we'll have to see when we get there. It's dinner, tomorrow."

I was unimpressed. Dinner out with little kids? How fun could it be? On the upside though, we might get a decent meal. I had to say I wasn't thrilled with what was coming out of the camp kitchen in our shed every night. Mum kept saying that things would be different once the house was built, that it was tricky to cook imaginatively with no facilities and hardly any fridge or bench space but to me it was just another sign that our family's standards were slipping. Actually, our standards were falling, tumbling, plummeting and cart wheeling off the edge of a cliff. Our family had no standards left. They'd all given up, packed their bags and moved away.

But I wasn't about to say anything. The week before,

when I criticised the re-heated stroganoff served with slightly stale bread, Mum yelled at me for about twenty minutes including telling me to stop being so ungrateful, to lose the attitude and to try cooking myself. Then she made me wash up. The yelling didn't have much effect but the cold, chunky, greasy water made me more careful about what I said at meals.

Dinner date night arrived and Dad had to pull himself away from his precious building work to come. I wasn't quite sure what he was doing out there all day with bits of string and pegs and a bunch of tools that measured stuff. Apparently it was something to do with foundations and a slab. So Josh told me, anyway.

"It's the most important part of the house," he said.

"You think?" I said. "For me, it's the colour of the paint on my bedroom walls. But, whatever."

I went out to take a look because I figured I should show a little bit of interest. I wasn't going to help build the thing but I could be magnanimous and make an appearance here and there. Unfortunately I tripped over a peg and got into trouble with Dad.

"Coco, no," he said. "Be careful. Muck it up and the house could fall down. Maybe you just need to go somewhere else right now."

*Fine*, I thought. *I'll go.* I still wasn't actually talking to Dad so I didn't answer him. But I did make a point of touching the peg with my toe before I ran away to get ready.

As it turned out, there was a benefit to going out, even to a nothing-special house in Budgong-in-the-middle-of-nowhere with no-one but tiny children to entertain me all evening. This was it: I got to dress up! It felt like breathing fresh air again to get out my suitcase and actually choose clothes that looked nice. For over a month there had been no one to impress and nothing to dress up for and I was feeling myself turning into a fashion-deprived has-been.

I dug down a few layers and carefully got out the new skinny jeans from my birthday. The shirt took a bit more thought. I had to try on at least eight before I settled on layering three tops over each other. Then I added some bling by pinning a massive silk rose to my shoulder and pulled my hair up into a messy bun. It's always surprising how long messy buns take to do. Sadly my white lace flats, which would have been perfect, were ruined. I'd had to chuck them out after the toilet debacle on the first day. But I had another pair in rose-coloured satin that I'd been saving for a special occasion.

"Ta-dah," I said, coming out from behind my curtain. "What do you think?" I did a twirl into the middle of the shed with a big smile on my face.

And then I saw Charlie.

The smile fell off my cheeks and onto the gravel floor.

"No way," I said. "You cannot wear that!"

I know that Charlie and I have always had different attitudes towards clothes, but let me just say that on this particular night she had reached a whole new level of low. When we lived in Sydney, she used to at least try to get it right. But what I saw in front of me was a frumpy, comfortable dag.

"What is that shirt?" I said, looking at something she used to wear to bed. And then, *horror!* "Are those Mum's jeans?"

"Yeah, they fit me," she said proudly. "They'll do, right?"

I gave her the full roll, Mum or no Mum.

"Charlie. If you ever have to ask if 'they'll do', you know that they definitely don't," I said. "It's a rule. The second rule is this: for the rest of your life, while you ever go out with me, and especially while either of us are still single, I will dress you."

She smiled cheerfully. "Whatever you say, oh great one. Dress me up."

The first thing to be replaced was the disgusting shirt. I gave her one of my own tops still laying on my bed.

"You should chuck this out. It's so over," I said, pulling the rejected shirt away from Charlie. She clung to it for a second but then relented and let me have it. I went to put it in the plastic bag of kitchen scraps but Dad grabbed it.

"No! We'll use it on the building site," he said. "Can always do with extra rags." He smiled at me but I shrugged and turned away.

"Come on, I'll do your hair," I said, ignoring Dad and turning back to Charlie. I sat down with her at my feet and plaited across the back of her head down into a side braid.

"That's much better," I said. "Here, put some makeup on."

She groaned back at me. "Really? I just can't be bothered."

"Please? For my sake? At least mascara. Come on." I pleaded with her. She grumbled but let me grab my makeup bag and half a minute later, sitting next to a candle for the light, I had a sister I wouldn't have been embarrassed to introduce to Saffron and Tiger and the girls. Well, not very embarrassed anyway.

With no proper mirror in the shed it was hard to get a full head-to-toe view, so I showed Charlie her polished face in the hand mirror.

"You're right," she said. "That's heaps better. I've kind of forgotten how to do it. You're so clever."

"It's what I do best," I said and examined my own make up. Yep, it was all smooth with no mascara blotches. I smiled experimentally to check the stretch on my lipstick but quickly closed my lips when I saw my teeth. Ick. *I must ask Mum when I can go to the dentist and fix all that*, I thought. *Definitely has to be before I go back to Sydney.*

"Hey Coco, let's take a picture," said Charlie. "You can use your iPod. Mum, can you do it?"

We stood together as Mum snapped away. "You girls look very nice," she said, just before Charlie made a silly face and held up her two fingers in a V.

"Ha ha, let me see that," I said. Charlie's eyebrow was raised and she looked almost manic. "If we had Facebook I'd post that, it's so funny."

"Imagine the loss to the world," said Josh. "We are all the poorer for not seeing your selfies on the internet."

I shrugged. The night after the 'getting sent out of the shed into the wild-horse-and-hokey-people-infested-paddock' incident, I had laid in bed and decided to try to learn to be cool with Josh. Do that thing where you heap burning coals on your enemy's head, whatever that means. Do unto others and so on and so forth. I knew I wouldn't succeed but I was determined to try. It wasn't worth all the hassle I was currently going through to keep reacting to his teasing.

"Whatever," I said and gave him a really cheesy grin, stretching my smile from ear to ear. I could see from his face he was just waiting for me to bite back so that he could come at me with the next insult, but when I didn't retaliate he looked surprised and stopped. Success! I thought, and nearly wrecked it by laughing at him. I stopped just in time and instead walked away with a secret smile.

"Are you guys ready?" Dad held the swinging kerosene lantern. (Yes, you read that right. Kerosene. Besides the candles, this was the only light source in our shed. I'm talking flammable fire hazards and unsafe, polluting chemicals. Plus the flames made dark black marks on the lantern glass and it was my job to clean them every day. And, despite all this, Dad still said, "Aaaah, this is the life," as he sat in the dark every night, trying to read the next chapter of his book, *Eco-tips for Renewable Resourcefulness; A Home Builders Manual* by P. Blah Blah Codswallop' by the light of the puny little kerosene flame, batting away the mosquitoes and drinking some sort of green tea concoction that he'd started on 'for antioxidants'. Seriously, the man became deranged when he took that redundancy. One of my next tactics, when and if I ever got to a library or, heaven forbid, to the internet, was to look up his symptoms and try to convince Mum to have him committed so we could get back to our normal lives.)

"Come on, we don't want to be late," said Mum. "Ness said six thirtyish and it's six thirty-five already."

"Doesn't the woman have a proper name?" I asked. "Isn't she Vanessa? What is with the whole 'Ness' thing? Does she like people to feel like they're being efficient, missing out on two actual syllables of her name?"

"Coco, just try to be nice please," said Mum, frowning. "Give the lady a chance. She's lovely, and we got on really well. It's very kind of her to invite us over. This is a great chance to get to know the neighbours. You guys might find some friends."

"Yeah, friends who are ten year-olds..." I muttered.

"I didn't say they were ten," said Mum, heating up.

"Coco!" said Dad. It was a warning. I ignored him.

"You said they were younger than us though," I said. "Ten, eight, four, two, what does it matter? We're hardly going to be friends, are we?"

Mum's face went tight. "Look, young lady. Skip the attitude please," she said. "I don't know what your problem is. You've been like this ever since we got here, and you're getting worse."

She put up her finger to wag in my face. "I know you didn't want to come. But we're here now, and nothing's changing for you for at least a year, so get used to it." She spat out her words like she could hardly control her voice.

I knew better than to challenge her, because, quite frankly, the idea of cleaning out that pit toilet made me vomit into my own mouth, plus my new resolution was to be cool, so I turned away but I couldn't stop a half eye roll spreading out over my face as I did.

"Onward and upward. Let's go out to dinner," I muttered under my breath.

But I made sure it was very, very quiet.

# CHAPTER 14

The clouds looked like rain as we got in the car. I had a half-thought that if it did start to sprinkle, my shoes might get muddy, but I dismissed it. Rain or no rain, there was no way I was turning up to dinner at the neighbours' crummy little farmhouse in gumboots. I was from the city. I'd show these bumpkins a thing or two.

As it turned out, the two words I picked to describe their farmhouse were completely off the mark. There was nothing crummy or little about Ness's stud farm.

For a start the driveway was actually a driveway. With proper gravel and everything. And it had no lumps or bumps. It was smooth. With a fence down both sides and two long rows of liquid amber trees that were just starting to drop their orange and yellow leaves.

*Okay*, I thought to myself. *So it's not as bad as I thought.* After we went through a big gate the driveway swung around to the right into a huge gravel-covered yard with a massive oak tree in the middle of it and a big shed-looking building off to one side. On the other side was a big weatherboard house with a massive wraparound veranda. Everything else was lush garden, green lawns and some pretty impressive autumn trees.

"Wow," said Charlie. "It's beautiful."

"You can probably see back to our shed from here," said Dad excitedly, looking to the right and nearly swerving into the fence. "Oh, no you can't. Sorry. But that's only because it's dark. When we build and get the solar panels up you'll be able to see the house." He was pointing to where he could see the slope down to the creek and some open space. "See there? That's one of our paddocks."

We pulled up and piled out of the car. This was looking good. Maybe it wouldn't be a complete write-off after all. My eyes took in the scene across the courtyard, from the house right over to the shed. Or, I should say, the stables. They had those half-door things that you see in kids' books about farms.

And half-doors always, always have horses behind them.

My heart went *flump*.

Inside the stables I could see some horses. Two horses, specifically. An enormous brown one and a very large white one.

*Uh oh,* I thought. And then, *double uh oh*. Because out of the open stable doors came two people. Two people I recognised. A brother and a sister, both with blond hair and blue eyes.

Mr Royal Easter Show and Miss Wrong Shirt.

There was nowhere to hide. And no way to back out. I briefly considered faking a stomach ache and demanding to be taken back to the farm, but Mum was already leading the way, "Hi, we're the Franks family.

You must be Ness's kids."

I hung back, avoiding shaking hands and trying to look like anybody else but myself.

"I'm Tessa," said the girl, who today was sporting jeans and a cheap top that could only have come from a very cheap shop.

"James," said the boy, who'd swapped his flanny for a surf shirt. *Better*, I thought, but then I looked at his feet and sighed. Still with the Cuban heels. *I guess you can't help what you are.*

Mum was pointing us out. "These are Charlie and Josh. You guys look about the same age. Fifteen, right? Good guess. And Tessa, you're, what, thirteen or fourteen?"

Blondie nodded and smiled. "Thirteen and a half."

Mum kept going. "And this," she said, turning around and looking for me, "is... where are you? Where've you gone? Ah, there you are." She pulled me out from behind Dad. "This is Coco."

I looked up and gave a half smile that kind of said, 'hey, who knew, right?' and I saw their faces turn from expectant and happy to doubtful and surprised. Tessa opened her eyes wide and looked at James, who just raised his eyebrows.

Mum was confused. "Have I missed something?" she said.

"We've met before," said James. He looked at me and shrugged.

Mum looked more confused. "You've met?"

"Yes. They rode through the property the other day," I said, trying to keep it all very calm and laid back.

"You didn't say anything about it," she said, but I

cut her off before she could get started. "Yeah, they've got these great horses," I said. "What were their names again?" I looked at James, daring him to contradict me.

"Our horses?" he said. "I don't think we introduced them properly." He gave me a look. I didn't know what it meant. "But you can come and see them now if you like."

"Absolutely," I said, smiling brightly and blinking. Charming was always a good option in uncomfortable situations. "They're so beautiful."

Mum's head was clearly still spinning but she followed everyone with Tessa and James back to the stables. As we reached the door I wrinkled up my nose. The smell coming from inside was strong enough to knock your socks off. *Or even your Cuban heels*, I thought. *Pity...*

But seriously. It was strong. Forget the pit toilet. That was nothing in comparison to this. Hang out with a bunch of big animals and their dung in a small space and you'll get a cast iron stomach.

I held my breath and plunged in through the doors. There were about eight horses in the stables all together. *I wonder how many kilos of poo that is per day?* I thought idly. *And who's supposed to clean it up?* But there was no time for idle thoughts. Tessa was showing us the horses.

In the first stall was a little Shetland pony, about the size of a very big dog. It was black and shiny with great big eyes and amazing lashes. And then the most surprising thing happened. The softy-teddy-loving part of me said *Awwww* and melted and all of a sudden I got it. I could finally see what horse-crazy nine year-olds and the whole *My Little Pony* industry were on about. This horse was cute. And the one next to it, a small brown and white pony, was also cute, with a mane that I just wanted to reach out and bury my face in.

Of course, I didn't let on. *Act cool. Be calm*, I told myself. *It's just a pony.*

"These are Sparky and Cuddles," said Tessa. "We used to ride them but we're obviously a bit big for them now. We keep them for the kids who come riding."

"What do you mean?" said Josh. His voice sounded really interested, and I noticed how close he was standing to Tessa.

"Didn't you know?" she said, smiling at him. (*Urgh* said my gross-out meter.) "We've got a horse riding business. We take people out for rides around the property — and sometimes on your property too. At least, we used to."

"Yeah," said James, chiming in. "We had an arrangement with the old owners." He looked directly at me so I gave him a half roll back. "There are some great rides around here. You can go right up into the national park, and then back to the river."

"The horses love it," said Tessa, gazing up at Josh. *Ick.* I wanted to puke. *Don't get married. Please, don't get married,* I thought. *I just cannot wear whatever disaster of a bridesmaid dress you would choose.*

With Tessa love-struck, James took the lead and showed us the rest of the horses. We met Nellie, Perry, Peach and Fozzles, all different colours and sizes and then finally we got to the two big, scary-looking beasts at the back. These were a whole different ballgame from the toy ponies at the front.

"This is Boldy," said James pointing to the white horse,

who nuzzled into his shoulder. Boldy was standing next to the big brown horse but when James reached out his hand for a pat, it gave him a nudge like it was saying 'go away' and then snorted and stamped its toe or paw or hoof or whatever it's called. I moved back a step and onto Tessa's foot.

"Sorry," I said, but she was already apologising to me.

"No, I'm sorry." She made a face at me. "Cupcake doesn't always like everyone. She's a bit hard to handle."

"Cupcake?" I said to James, who somehow was standing right beside me now. He was close enough that I could hear him breathe. "You ride a horse called Cupcake?" I giggled.

He looked at me and for a second his bright blue eyes took my breath away. But then I saw his expression—disappointed.

"Whatever, Coco," he said. "Come ride with us some time. If you want." He shrugged and turned away but as he did something else surprising happened.

A part of my stomach turned over, burst into tears and curled up in a ball. I tried to squash the feeling of smallness away and not care, but for some reason that I didn't understand, I did care. *This isn't supposed to happen*, I thought. *I'm better than him. This is embarrassing. And a bit weird.*

And then it got even weirder. *I'm going to cry! Because a guy I don't even like doesn't approve of me!* My face turned red and my eyes start to well up and I started rubbing at them with my wrist.

"You okay, Coco?" said Mum, a puzzled look on her face. "Your eyes look all red."

"Maybe I'm allergic to hay," I said hurriedly, looking away. "I'll go stand outside."

I walked away from the group. Behind me Charlie was oohing and aahing over Fozzles ("I love piebalds! They're so cute," she said over and over) and everyone was reaching out their hands, having a pat of Boldy and Nellie and Perry and Barry and Harry or whatever their names were. No one was game to pat Cupcake.

The tears were still threatening and I decided I needed some space and some peace so I headed for the side door, out to the garden. I could feel the fresh air on my face as I got closer to the entrance and ignored Tessa who was calling out something to me about watching out.

*At last,* I thought, *some privacy!* And I took a step out into the garden.

I should not have ignored Tessa.

What she had said was, "Watch out. There's a massive puddle outside the door."

It would have been wise to listen.

Because the puddle wasn't just water. It was mud, mixed with horse poo. And I was in it. I looked down at my shirt which was now splashed with brown drops, and then down at my feet, which were nowhere to be seen. The mud had squished up past my ankles and into my jeans and completely covered my pink satin flats.

I was stuck.

If my life was a movie, this would have been the perfect scenario for the good looking and charming but slightly accident-prone heroine (ie. me) to meet Ness, the classy neighbour.

I'm beginning to think that maybe something's going

on without me realising it because yes, you guessed it. Right then Ness appeared.

"Hi, I'm Ness," said Ness (obviously). She was big and smiley with curly hair and she was wearing head to toe horse gear. Jodhpurs, a button down shirt and a massive big vest. She stuck out her hand at me so I went to shake it but she laughed. "No. I'm pulling you out."

I grabbed her hand, feeling silly, and came out of the swamp.

"So sorry. We really must get that hole filled in with gravel. Let's get you something to wear," said Ness. Her voice was kind. "You're covered. Come on into the house and I'll fix you up."

I hardly wanted to speak because I still felt like crying so I sniffled and shuffled along behind her and then she hugged me and for some reason I felt so safe and warm and cared for, like I hadn't felt in months, that I did everything she said, even when it involved taking off most of my muddy clothes on the veranda (she politely averted her eyes), cleaning off in the laundry and putting on an indescribable purple something of Tessa's (ugh) that she brought out to me.

"That colour really suits you," she said, looking at me once I'd cleaned up and changed. "I bet you wear that a lot. Purple brings out your eyes."

"No," I said. I shrugged. "I don't have anything purple. I used to wear it all the time but Samantha said..." and my voice trailed off. "I mean, I kind of went off it for a while."

"Well, you should go back to it," said Ness. "It's great on you."

I guess everyone else would have called the evening a success. We ate lamb stew and a chocolate, self-saucing pudding which were yum by anyone's standard. Mum and Dad talked non-stop to Ness about the land, horses, farming and driveways, and James and Tessa talked non-stop to Josh and Charlie. A couple of times I tried to join in their conversation but no-one seemed to hear anything I said—they just talked over me—so I ate and listened and felt small and insignificant and sorry for myself in someone else's clothes.

After dinner the kids (except me) took themselves off to hang out in James' room while I sat in with Mum and Dad and Ness, pretending I didn't want to be part of it, and looking instead at Ness's jam-packed, overflowing bookshelves. As I listened to the laughing coming from down the hall I suddenly felt sad. And low. And (here I surprised myself for a third time that evening) lonely.

It was weird. I hadn't changed my mind; I still didn't want to be in Budgong. I wanted to go back to Sydney. And I was determined not to like Tessa and James, who were daggy and hokey and not up to my standards. Plus James seemed so boring and straightforward. He obviously couldn't stand me, and I wasn't going to hang out with someone who wasn't on my wavelength.

But that wasn't the main problem.

I suddenly realised I still wanted friends—at least for now. Once I got back to Sydney I could pick up where I left off, but it's hard to be in a place where there's absolutely no-one who likes you and no one you like.

Especially not for a whole year.

# CHAPTER 15

For the next whole entire month I was lonely and bored. Josh called me a sook and even though I got mad at him, I knew he wasn't far off being right. I was more than sorry for myself. I was pathetic.

Charlie and Josh now had a new way to fill their afternoons — riding with Tessa and James. After only about two lessons on how to hold the reins and direct a horse they saddled up and hopped on, never to hop off again. It was like they'd been born up there. Charlie rode Fozzles, Tessa was on Boldy and Josh and James rode Nellie and Perry. Charlie started wearing jodhpurs and boots all day and these weird looking things — 'chaps' I think they're called — that got strapped around her legs.

"You're just wearing that stuff to annoy me," I said, complaining.

She gave me a look. "Yeah, like I choose my outfits each day specifically with you in mind," she said. "Anyway, what's wrong with it?" She looked down at her riding vest and brushed off a few brown hairs.

"You smell like horse," I said. "And it's gross to have animal hair all over you."

"But it's fun to ride," she said. "You should try it."

I didn't try it. I watched instead, sulking and miserable, from the shed as they galloped across the paddocks, set up jumps and took the horses down to the creek.

The night we went over to Ness's place Mum and Dad had (of course) given Tessa and James unlimited permission to ride on our property.

"That sounds terrific!" said Mum. "Come any time." Dad had smiled along. I hadn't looked over at James because I knew he'd be looking at me and I could feel my face already starting to burn so I'd pretended to be engrossed in one of Ness's old Phantom comics until they went back to planning their first ride.

"You should come," Charlie said that night and Tessa agreed. "Yeah, come. We're going up this awesome cliff face. The view is incredible."

"Not really my thing, but thanks," I said, and on the day they went I stayed in the shed and played an old version of Angry Birds on my iPod. There's something about smashing up cartoon pigs that's strangely satisfying when you're annoyed.

Charlie came in every night exhausted and with an irritatingly happy face. Her new favourite thing in the evening was to sit with her feet resting on the log stove (it was getting cold) and talk about horses. Boldy played up today, Nellie's starting to pigroot, Perry jumped higher than he's ever gone before, blah blah blah. I studiously ignored it and changed the subject as necessary, but sometimes she'd make a special effort and try to persuade me to join in.

"You're ridiculous, you know that, right?" she said

once, lying on my bed and sticking her feet into my doona to keep warm.

I shrugged. "I just know what I don't like doing. And I don't like horses or riding, so I'm not going to start."

"But you haven't even tried it," she groaned. "It's like when we were little and you wouldn't eat cheesecake because you couldn't imagine how cheese and cake would taste nice together. You missed out on like four whole years worth of amazing deliciousness because you wouldn't even put a teaspoon of it on your tongue."

"That's completely different," I said. "I just didn't get the whole concept of cream cheese. But I know what horses are like and what they do. It's not as if I'd suddenly go, 'oh, I get it, they run along the ground. I always thought they flew'."

"Whatever," she said. "You're just missing out on heaps of fun. And I'm missing you." She made a sad, pouty face. "Anyway, even if you didn't like the horse bit of it, you could still just hang out with us all."

"What? Tessa and James?" I said. I made a face imitating Tessa's long nose and James' serious look. "Come on."

"No, they're really nice," she said. But she was laughing. "That's funny, but you're mean. Tessa's sweet and James has an awesome sense of humour."

"Really? He seems so..." I searched for the right word, "...dull."

"He says what he thinks," said Charlie. "And he doesn't play games. He is who he is. But he's hilariously funny when he wants to be. And he'll do anything. He's fearless."

"You're in love," I said accusingly.

"Who with?" She looked shocked.

"James."

"Are you kidding? No way! Seriously, I'm not. But I think Tessa's in love with Josh a bit."

"Ewww. How could she be?" I said. "But anyway. They don't like me." I shrugged. "It wouldn't be fun."

"They only don't like you because you're kind of too cool for them—or you act that way at least," she said. "If you just came out with us they'd see the real you." She thought for a moment. "Well, Tessa would anyway. Maybe James still wouldn't like you."

"He hates me," I said, thinking about it for a second. "But then, I kind of hate him too." I suddenly got sick of the conversation. "Anyway, I just don't want to. I just don't want to like that kind of stuff. I don't want to spend my days getting hot and sweaty and tramping through the mud."

"But the horses do all the tramping for you." It was her last-ditch effort but I wasn't going to be moved.

"You know what I mean," I said. "It's icky. Sorry. But I'm just not interested. And I'm not going to learn to be. Now give me my doona back." I pulled the doona off her warm feet so she kicked me and I jumped on her and soon we were giggle-wrestling which was awesome fun, at least until Dad told us to stop it, we were being way too noisy and Mum said the same thing she's said for the past thirteen years which is, 'be careful or it'll all end in tears.'

It occurred to me that night that if Charlie really did miss me as much as she said she did she should suggest to everyone else that they hang out with me in the shed instead of riding and I almost felt happy thinking about it as I went to sleep. Maybe things wouldn't be so bad tomorrow. Maybe everyone would make an effort to include me and take care of me. Maybe even James would be nice. I could imagine him laughing and chatting with me. Maybe I might be able to have some fun in the part of the year that was left before I went back to Sydney.

But there's something about the middle of the night that completely messes up your perception of reality because the next day everything was back to what it had been. Dad was still building his muddy little house, Mum was still washing and cooking and trying to teach us maths and science, Josh was still teasing me and Charlie was still horse-crazy.

I watched as my brother and sister and their new friends took off on a ride over the mountain and waited, kicking my feet, for the three long, boring hours it took for them to come back. There are only so many times you can play Angry Birds, and anyway, I'd finished all the levels.

As the afternoon sky got darker, it seemed to match my thoughts which were going from mildly annoyed to completely depressed and desperate.

*No one really cares about me. If they did, they wouldn't have brought me here. I can't believe I'm reduced to living in what's practically the outback with no friends and no one who even likes me just a tiny bit. My clothes are dirty, my shoes are ruined, my nice stuff is in storage and I can't even take a shower. I hate everyone. I wish they'd all just disappear and leave me alone. Waaah.*

The only place for me was bed. I put myself under my doona and then refused to get up for dinner, refused to talk to Charlie when she came in gasping with delight about the amazing ride she'd just been on, refused (of course) to answer Dad when he asked me if I was okay and refused to bring in wood for the fireplace.

"I don't feel well," I kept repeating, looking at the wall. "I just feel sick." Actually, I just felt angry. And sad. But I mostly didn't feel like arguing any more. It was easier to lie down.

*Something has to change*, I thought to myself as I lay there, listening to everyone eat and laugh and bicker and live. *Stuff can't be like this for much longer or I don't know what I'm going to do.*

I didn't know that the change was already on its way. And it was something that would take me completely by surprise.

While Charlie and Josh had been hanging out with Tessa and James, Mum had been spending time with Ness. And it was firing her up. I'd never heard her talk so enthusiastically as when she was explaining Ness's dilemma to Dad.

"Her problem is that they don't have enough land for all the horses they want. They've got the stables, and of course they do those rides, but she's constantly getting people ringing and emailing to ask if they can let their horses live at her place, you know — agistment — but they don't have the space. I was thinking though. We do! We could agist."

"Even if we did it until we work out what else we can do with the property, that would solve some cash flow problems," Dad said, thinking. And then he got all enthusiastic as well. "We'd need to make sure the fencing was secure, obviously. And we'd have to talk to Ness about setting it up so the horses all have what they need, and so the business side was okay, but we could get it going pretty much straight away."

A few weeks later, horses moved onto our property. There were just three to begin with. I was bored and Charlie was out so I walked down to the end paddock with Mum to see them come off the float. They were quiet at first but after their halters were taken off they kicked and squealed and shook their heads. And then they ran and ran, like it was the first time they'd been free in years. They looked around at the field and at each other and I could almost see horsey joy on their faces.

*Huh,* I thought. *It's a nice place. For them. Not so much for me.*

Over the next few weeks more horses came in their floats down our mountain track. Soon we had over twenty spread over three paddocks. Mum and Charlie spent days out looking at them, feeding them, trying to remember their names and getting to know their quirks.

And then one morning, while everyone else was busy or out, a horse turned up that I already knew.

It was Cupcake.

Ness brought her over. "Hey Coco, are you the only one here?" she called out, sticking her head in the door of the shed. "Can you let your mum know I'm putting her in the paddock with the others? I think she's stressed out from being in the stables — a bit barn-sour — and she's gotten too hard to handle. I've really got to spend more time with her in the ring but I'm flat chat for the next few months and I won't get to it. So until I figure out what else to do with her, she'll just have to spend more time with the herd."

I hopped out of bed and walked down with Ness to the horse float. Finally something interesting was happening in this boring, boring place.

It wasn't that I was into Cupcake, although it did seem like she had a bit more personality and a few more opinions than the other horses. It was more that I liked Ness. She had the same blue eyes as James, which I've always said were particularly good-looking eyes but as well as that, there was an aliveness and enthusiasm about her. It was kind of intriguing, but also slightly embarrassing. It was like she didn't care what other people thought so she just said whatever she was thinking out loud. She didn't seem worried about what she might look like or how she came across. She just looked free.

And happy.

Cupcake, on the other hand, wasn't happy. She neighed and bucked as she was led out of the float.

"Stand up," said Ness, putting a hand on her neck but it didn't work. Cupcake looked angry and nothing anyone did was going to help. She snorted hot air and tossed her head and rolled her eyes.

It was when I saw the eye roll that everything changed. You'd think that a horse and a girl would look nothing alike, but as soon as I saw her do what I'd been doing for months, it was like I recognised myself.

And then I couldn't help it. I didn't usually put my hand out to pat horses, but I had this huge intense feeling inside me. I wanted to let Cupcake know that it was okay. I wanted her to know that I understood how she felt. I was desperate to tell her that I felt the same.

I put my hand out. And it was like I'd put on sound blocking headphones. Everything went very quiet. Cupcake looked at me and her body relaxed and she stopped fussing. Even the birds and the crickets subsided into silence. I touched Cupcake's neck and felt the warm of her coat. She turned her head around to me and I could feel her breath on my hands and a strange tickly feel of her nostrils.

She was suddenly quiet and happy.

And it was because of me.

"She really likes you, Coco," said Ness, quietly. "Look. She's calmed right down."

I looked up at Ness. "Do you think so?" My eyes were wide and I actually felt excited.

"I'm sure so. It's definitely you. She's been terrible to everyone else. Tessa and James have given up on her. And Charlie just about got bucked off when she tried to ride her last week. But she looks like she's bonded with you."

A thrill went from the ends of my hair all the way into my body and through to my toenails. I'd never felt anything like it. Well, maybe that one time when Mum let me sit and watch the parades in the Queen Victoria Building in Australian Fashion Week when I was four. Seeing those models in such amazing outfits had given me a tingle that had been unmatched by anything else in the world, ever. At least, up until now.

"Why don't you walk her down to the paddock?" Ness

said. She handed me the lead rope that was attached to Cupcake's halter.

"Really? I've never done that before," I said. I didn't want to, but I did want to, and I didn't know what to do.

"It's easy," said Ness. "You just walk."

I started out tentatively tugging at the rope but then Ness showed me how to hold it, with more authority, showing her that I was the boss, and then I was walking and Cupcake was walking beside me and the two of us were walking together like, I don't know, like we were friends. *If you can be friends with a horse*, I thought. Because, I know, I know, it sounded ridiculous. But maybe it was true. Maybe Cupcake and I were friends.

Cupcake went into the paddock, running with the herd and after giving me a hug, Ness left and then I hummed and buzzed around by myself with something brimming up inside me that I hadn't felt for ages. Maybe it was hope? Or joy? I'm not sure. All I know is that it sounded like zing and felt like a bouncy ball and tasted a little like honey.

"You're very chirpy today," said Dad over dinner. I smiled widely and opened my mouth but the zing and the bounce weren't quite enough to break my 'don't-talk-to-Dad' rule so I stayed quiet. He looked a bit deflated and I actually felt sorry for him.

Mum changed the subject. "Where did you guys ride today?" she asked, talking to Charlie and Josh. "Which horse were you on?"

I nearly even listened as Charlie explained about Perry and having to change saddles because it didn't fit her girth and about this amazing track that just went straight up behind the property. And I nearly even paid attention to what Josh said about the funny thing that Tessa did while he was riding behind her but all the time I was buzzing and zinging and humming inside, thinking to myself, *I took Cupcake for a walk and I'm the special person for her and she calmed down just for me because she liked me,* but then the honey taste in my mouth turned to vinegar when I heard Charlie say this:

"Did Ness bring Cupcake over? She said she doesn't know what she's going to do with her if she can't get her to settle down. She might have to sell her."

I choked. And then coughed. And then choked again.

"Are you alright, Coco?" Mum looked really concerned. She leaned over to pat me on the back but I pushed her hand away.

"No no, I'm okay," I almost squealed. "No. Tell me about Cupcake. Would Ness really sell her? Would she do that? She can't."

I stopped to find the whole family gazing at me with slightly odd looks. My words, overdone and loud, echoed around me and then fell out of the air to the floor. I could hear the tiny smashing noises of concern on concrete. I felt awkward. This was embarrassing.

Charlie looked at me with interest. "Yeah. She might sell Cupcake. That's what she said." She narrowed her eyes, still trying to figure me out. "Did you see her when they came down today?"

I shrugged and held my breath. "A bit." I didn't want to give too much away. But it didn't matter anyway. Charlie was off on another topic with bright, enthusiastic eyes.

"Did she tell you about Pony Camp?" she said. "It sounds like heaps of fun. About twenty five people come, all around our age, and some bring horses and some ride the ones here, but it's three days and we camp and go on day-long rides and even a beach ride and sometimes swimming in the river with the horses."

Dad looked up. "When's it on? The house might be ready by then. Maybe we'll be able to help, or everyone could camp on the property?"

"Tessa said it's in late spring, early summer," said Josh. "It sounds awesome."

I breathed again. The conversation moved on to camp and beyond. But the buzz and the zing and humming inside me had turned to a churning worry. Would Cupcake be sold? Would they send her away? Would I lose, once again, the only friend I had?

I didn't know what I was going to do.

I only knew I had to do something.

# CHAPTER 16

Up to this point, every afternoon I had lain on my bed, watching Charlie and Josh get their gear on to go out on with Tessa and James and listening to Mum yell, "Have you got a helmet on? Have you got a mobile phone just in case?"

Every afternoon I'd heard Josh yell back, "There's no point, because nothing's going to happen and some places don't even get reception."

And every afternoon I'd seen Mum run out and give them a phone anyway. "I don't care. Take the phone. It's Ness's rule and there'll be somewhere you can go to get yourself a signal."

"Well if I fall off and break my leg I'll try to do it in a place with good reception," yelled Charlie as she rode away.

"Just take the phone, Charlie," said Dad, but he was laughing.

The day after Cupcake arrived, I waited until they'd gone out and until Mum and Dad were looking at house plans and concrete specs. Then I snuck out of my bed and looked around for some shoes and a jacket. I was going down to the paddock.

To begin with I just hung over the side of the fence and watched Cupcake in a big group of horses all eating grass. It looked pretty boring. *She probably wants something more interesting to eat,* I thought, so I ran back and stole a couple of carrots from the kitchen.

To get to Cupcake I realised I'd have to climb the fence. Which is easier said than done in ballet flats, let me tell you. Especially when you're holding carrots. I won't say I fell, but I won't say that it was a seamless, graceful descent down from the timber palings. Plus I may have got a splinter in my thumb that hurt a lot and I may also have looked down at my jeans and seen grass stains on the knees.

But I was over, and no one had seen me and there was no potential for embarrassment, unless of course horses laugh about humans when they're on their own, but that's really not even worth thinking about. Besides, I was sure Cupcake wouldn't laugh at me. Especially once she'd seen that I had carrots.

At first the other horses crowded around. They were warm and their noses were surprisingly velvety and once I got used to the smell it wasn't icky at all, but they weren't the ones I had come to see. It took a little while to work out how to walk between them all (*Do you avoid the back legs? Will they squash me like a caterpillar? Am I going to die?*) but I made it to Cupcake and held out my carrot. At first she shook her head and made a little 'heh heh heh' sound deep and low, but I said, "It's okay, it's just me," and stood there quietly and after she'd looked at me for about two seconds, she slowly put her head down and let me give her a pat. And then I stood next to her, holding out the carrot and laughing and trying not to get grossed out while her big, slobbery mouth took it off my outstretched hand and crunched it up.

The next day I went down again. This time though, instead of slipping on my ballet flats I snuck on a pair of Charlie's boots instead. *It's only so it's easier to climb the fence,* I said to myself. *Definitely not a fashion statement.* The day after that I found some old, grubby jeans as well. *Can't wreck my good stuff,* I justified to myself.

By the end of the week Cupcake would run to the fence when she saw me walking down and nudge me under my arm as I climbed over. Soon I was able to put my arms around her neck and then she started rubbing her forehead on my back. I had to make sure I brushed the hair off my shirt before Charlie got back so she wouldn't find out what I was doing, although I guess you could have made the argument that Charlie wouldn't actually notice if there was horse hair on anyone's shirt. But I wasn't taking any chances. The last thing I wanted was for my family to start pushing me towards 'having fun' and riding and joining in with the whole community bonding thing. I was going to do things my way and in my time.

I watched carefully but sneakily one day as Charlie put a halter on Fozzles. It looked easy enough. *Clip here, don't undo that bit, slip it over the nose.* That afternoon I grabbed one from the side of the shed where Mum now had about six or eight hanging on hooks, hid it under my jumper and went down the paddock.

As I climbed the fence with Cupcake nudging me I

pulled out the halter. "Come on Cupcake," I said, "Put this on." But I was too loud and too quick and she shied and ran away from me. That day I couldn't even get her back with a carrot. It took me a week of carrying the halter and the carrot together every day so she could see it and get used to it before I was able to put it on her. I felt like a fumble fingers wobbling around with clips and catches but Cupcake was calm and patient with me and she let me do it. Every day. We'd put it on, have a walk together and then she'd have a carrot and I'd give her a scratch and take it all off again.

A few weeks later I saw Ness attach a long rope to the halter and walk Cuddles around her in circles. So I grabbed a rope, stuffed it under my shirt and headed off down the paddock. Cupcake came when I offered her a carrot and it was easy to put on her halter and then she obligingly walked around in a circle for me.

I was so excited I didn't hear Ness walk up behind me.

"I didn't think you liked horses," she said.

I wheeled around, guilty faced.

"No, keep going," she said. "I want to see what you can do."

At the sound of Ness's voice Cupcake put her ears back and pulled away, but I turned to her and said, "It's okay. You're okay." Once she could see that I was calm, she calmed down too and kept walking.

Ness came up quietly and stood next to me. "Can you get her to trot?" she said.

"How do I do that?" I asked.

"Click your mouth and say 'trot'. She knows the

commands. She just needs to hear them said with authority. You're in charge."

I shifted my body language like I was being bossy, puffed out my chest, clicked my tongue and told her to 'trot'. Immediately Cupcake read my signals and began trotting around me. I glanced at Ness, excited. She gave me a smile.

"Now make her stop," said Ness. "Again, like you mean it."

"Wo-oah," I said strongly, and Cupcake came to a halt.

"Why are you doing this?" Ness said. She was quiet, keeping things calm. "Seriously, I didn't think you liked horses."

"I don't," I said. "It's just Cupcake. I don't know. There's something..."

"You two have a connection," she said. She was staring at me and her blue eyes seemed brighter in the sun. "You understand each other." Her voice raised a few notes in excitement. "It happens sometimes. Horses and people aren't so different, you know. Some horses are exclusive about who they like and don't like, just like people. This one hates most people, but she loves you. You're her leader. She'll follow you anywhere if you lead her. You've got a friend."

I looked at Cupcake, clicked my mouth and got her to trot again. Her brown eyes caught mine and I'll swear I almost saw her wink.

"Charlie said you were going to sell her," I said. My voice sounded hard.

"It's a possibility. I just don't have the time for her."

Ness shrugged. "She's a great horse, but she needs work."

"Could I do it? The work, I mean. Take the time? Get her settled?" I stopped the trot and turned to Ness, desperate. Cupcake stood and watched us both.

"But you don't know how to do it." Ness looked at me doubtfully. "It's quite a thing."

"But I could learn. You could teach me. And then I could learn to ride her too. If I did the work you wouldn't have to sell her..."

Ness narrowed her eyes and looked into the distance, but then she smiled and looked at me. "Yeah. Okay. Why not?" She shrugged. "We can see how it goes. I'll teach you. You teach her. But you have to do exactly what I say because I know what I'm doing. And also you've got to do it every day. You can't give up next week or she'll just go backwards."

"You don't have to worry about that," I said. "I've been coming down every day for weeks already."

"I know," said Ness.

"You do?"

"Yeah. Don't forget, I can see this paddock from my place. I've been watching."

My face went red. "I didn't want to tell anyone."

"I get that," she said, shrugging. "Some things need to be kept to yourself for a while."

"Yeah," I said. "I still don't really want to tell anyone though. Would it be too much... Would you mind if... Could you keep this all a secret? I want to surprise them."

She looked at me knowingly.

"You like to be a bit special, don't you."

"What do you mean?"

"I mean, well, let's see," she said. "How can I put it. There's a phrase in Pride and Prejudice—you've read that, right?"

I nodded, offended. "Of course. It's like, only the second best book in the whole world."

"Well, there's a bit where Elizabeth says to Darcy something like this: 'You and I are both alike. We both don't want to say anything unless it will amaze the whole room'." She looked me, grinning. "I'm a little bit the same. And James is the exact opposite. He hates show and game-playing. He'd rather say it straight out. But I think you like to amaze the room."

I looked down, slightly affronted. "I guess." I shrugged my shoulders. "I just don't want to be ordinary."

"What's wrong with ordinary?" Ness asked. She seemed genuinely curious.

I made a face. "It's so... embarrassing. Especially when Charlie's so not ordinary. Everyone always says how talented and how pretty and how, I don't know, how everything she is."

Ness raised her eyebrows. "Really? Because I would have thought you guys were both pretty similar in that way. Both talented I mean. And pretty, of course. Aren't you kind of the same?"

"Yeah, but you haven't seen her at school. She's smart, sporty and arty and she has those amazing eyelashes. And even worse, she doesn't even care about it. Everyone just likes her. I have to try harder at everything."

Ness thought for a moment. She pulled Cupcake in a bit closer.

"I'll tell you something that you'll think I'm just saying because I want you to feel better, but that's not the reason I'm saying it."

I looked up at her. "What?"

"Charlie is Charlie. You are you. You're different people. She has something special about her, that's true. But you do too."

"Yeah, but she has like ten — no, a hundred — special things about her." I said. "I have only one thing I'm good at. I can do clothes."

"One thing? I think you'll find there's a lot more than just one thing," said Ness. "But even if it is just one thing, it's actually two." She pointed to Cupcake who was rubbing her head on my back. "You've got a compassion about you that's special. Animals can see it. It's a kind of innocence."

"Innocence?" I looked at her strangely. "That doesn't sound good. That sounds lame."

"No," she said. "No, it's beautiful. It's a beauty in your soul. It's a gift of love. Horses know when you've got it."

"Well, Mum would say I haven't been very loving recently," I said, turning down my mouth. I kicked my toe in the dirt. "And I haven't spoken a word to Dad since we moved. That's like six months or something now. Maybe I've got a gift of hate — not love."

"Oh, Coco," she said. Her voice sounded funny. Wobbly, kind of. She looked at me. "That's not hate. You're just angry."

Cupcake was standing between Ness and I and it was just as well because as soon as she said it my eyes started to fill up.

*Great. I don't want to cry in front of Ness*, I thought. *Even more embarrassing*. I made my eyes as big as I could trying to keep the tear drops inside but first one, then the other, leaked and in about a minute I had wet, streaky cheeks. I kept my face away from Ness and towards Cupcake but it was too late. She'd already noticed.

"Hey, it's okay," she said. "Everyone gets angry. I've been pretty mad myself at different times. The thing is to do something with your anger. You don't want to let it make you bitter."

"But how can I help that?" I said, wiping the drips off my cheeks. My voice sounded wobbly and silly. "I'm always going to be angry with Dad. I just don't think I can forgive him for making us move. I just hate it here." I started combing out Cupcake's mane with my fingers, just to do something with my hands. "No offence. I like you and all that—in fact, you're probably the only person I do like. It's just I didn't want to leave Sydney."

Ness looked at me. Her eyes were softer and they looked kind.

"No offence taken, Coco. I know how you feel. I do. It's really hard to lose your home."

*But that's not the real problem*, I suddenly thought.

And then I knew what the real problem was. I understood the real reason why I was angry.

"Actually, no. It's not even that. I'm mostly mad because no one paid any attention to me, to the fact that I didn't want to go," I said fiercely. My voice went from wobble to wild. "It was like, no, it still is... like being in one of those bad dreams where you're trying to yell but nothing comes out of your mouth. From the very first day — and it was my birthday too — they just didn't listen to a single thing I said."

Cupcake started to shift her weight back and forth. "Sorry," I said, quiet again. "Sorry, Cupcake. I didn't mean to upset you. I'll stay calm now, okay?"

Ness stood still. She took a deep breath and then she let it out.

"Yeah," she said. "I get it. When no one listens to you, that is hard. That's the hardest thing of all."

So Ness and I started our secret horse training. First we worked in the round yard with Cupcake once a week and then I practiced what I'd learned with her every afternoon when Josh and Charlie were out riding. When Cupcake got calmer and heaps more predictable and when I felt confident, Ness came over to give me riding lessons.

"Heels down, chin up, sit on your pockets, keep your hands below your belly button. No, not up like that. You're not in a Wild West movie! Don't be scared. You're in charge."

But I was never scared. Not even for a second. My tummy wobbled slightly when I first got up, just because it looked like a long way down, but I trusted Cupcake and she trusted me. We were learning together.

"You can ride, you know," said Ness, two months later. "You're good. You're steady, you're confident and you've got style. In fact, you've got a better natural seat than Charlie. I think you were made for this."

"Do you think I'm ready?" I asked her.

"I think you're ready," she said.

A few days later I casually mentioned to Charlie that

I might join her on a ride that afternoon.

"You're going up to the dam, right?" I said. "So, I might come today."

She raised her eyebrows. "Really? That would be cool."

"Great."

"We can go a bit slow if you like."

"Meh. Whatever. I'll try to keep up."

"Okay." She looked at me like I was about to let her into the joke. "You're serious, right?"

"Yeah," I said, making wide eyes at her. "Have I ever joked about going riding before?"

"Well... I guess not."

"So, then," I shrugged.

"So, then." She looked at me and laughed. "We're going at three thirty."

"Like usual, right? If you go over to the stables to saddle up with Josh, I'll meet you there."

"Okay." She looked confused. "Um, which horse do you want to take? You could go on Nellie. She's pretty good for beginners."

"Don't worry about that," I said mysteriously. "I'll just see you there. Three thirty."

"Okay." She was curious and her eyes narrowed. "See you there..."

Let me just say that, in life, the element of surprise is vastly underrated.

When I galloped down James and Tessa's driveway on Cupcake, and then wheeled around and pulled her up, you could have caught ten dozen flies in everyone's open mouths. It took about five seconds for any words to come out at all, and then:

"Is that you, Coco?" said Tessa.

"Is that Cupcake?" said Josh.

"You can ride?" said Charlie.

"You can ride Cupcake?" said James.

I shrugged, enjoying myself. "Aaah. I took a couple lessons. No big deal, right? So, are you guys ready or what? Let's go."

It was James' eyes that looked the longest and shone the brightest. He didn't say anything, but he rode next to me all the way.

# CHAPTER 17

I didn't want to say it or even think it, but life got better. I wasn't admitting to anything but everyone noticed the difference. I was out of bed, I had more energy and I had something to look forward to. It was nice to feel more normal. I did better in my school work, ate more and laughed almost every day. I even helped around the shed and did some fetching and carrying for Dad. I watched the frame of the new house go up. It was kind of fun.

Obviously, though, I didn't want anyone to take 'new happy light-hearted Coco' for granted or to forget that I had been dragged there against my will, so I made sure I mentioned going to back to Sydney at least once a day. For example:

Mum: "What a beautiful sunset tonight." Me: "Yes, it's gorgeous. I'll almost miss the sunsets when I go back to Sydney next year."

Charlie: "Doing school at home gives me heaps more time to myself." Me: "I know. It's cool, right? I'll have to make the most of it now before I go back to Sydney next year."

Josh: "Nice soup, Mum. Delish." Me: "It's great. I

wonder what boarding school food will be like when I go back to Sydney next year?" Josh: "Would you just shut up already?"

The best part of being happier was that finally, I had friends. Tessa turned out to be nice, even though she was shy and still wore all the wrong shirts, but she wanted to learn and a few times when I helped her with her clothes she was so grateful—and she looked so good—that I actually felt pretty proud of myself, like I'd done something nice.

"When I get back to Sydney next year I'll buy you something at the place I always used to get my jeans," I said. "Something in a really pale blue. It will go with your eyes."

Tessa giggled and preened a little, especially once I put some make up on her.

"See? That really helps." I stood back to admire my work. "There's no reason why anyone should ever go out anywhere without mascara and eyeliner on."

"What about just down to the stables?" Tessa asked. Her face was worried.

"Look, obviously you can do what you like," I said. "I'm just saying, you don't know when or where someone might see you—or who it will be. So it's best to be prepared, right? It takes about two minutes to put on, and you never know—if you meet someone who turns out to be the boy of your dreams, it might be the most useful two minutes of your life."

Tessa giggled and then blinked a few times. "My eyes feel weird. Is that normal?"

"You'll get used to it," I said. "What's that phrase?

You have to suffer to be beautiful."

With her eyes watering, Tessa was suffering. But she did look beautiful.

"You have used your powers for good," said Charlie later in her Yoda voice, being silly. But she was happy with me for being nice to her friend. And Josh approved too. He was still hanging around Tessa like a lost puppy. That romance was doing my head in. Mostly because I couldn't imagine anyone liking my brother. I mean, really? Thankfully it wasn't like they were about to start kissing around every corner. Even though Tessa giggled and looked at him all the time, neither of them seemed to have the guts to do anything about it. Instead they just talked about horses. Incessantly. Boringly. Never-endingly.

Even though I now loved riding, and we all went out together on the horses just about every afternoon, it wasn't like horses had taken over my world like they had for Charlie and Josh.

For me, it was about one horse. I loved Cupcake.

The more time I spent with her, the more I realised that she was probably the closest friend I had ever had, which sounds ridiculous, I know, because she was an animal, obviously, and not a person. But it was like we both knew each other so well and trusted each other so much that nothing could go wrong.

What I loved was that we could be—no, we *had* to be—completely honest with each other. There was no mistaking how she was feeling. Horses don't play games or hide things. And they're amazing at picking up on your feelings too. When I was worried, she got worried.

When I was excited, her ears pricked up and she went faster. If I was angry I had to make sure I got rid of it and truly calmed down before I could work with her.

Cupcake responded to me like no one else. I was definitely her favourite person. We spent at least two hours together every day, either riding or in the round yard, and at the end I made sure she always had a bucket of feed ready.

And it was making a huge difference. She had calmed down a lot, even to the point where other (carefully chosen) people could ride her again. But mostly everyone just said, "Oh, Cupcake is pretty much Coco's horse."

It did worry me that once I went back to Sydney in February I'd miss her and she'd be left alone, but I tried to put it out of my mind. Besides, I figured that if I spent enough time with her now, she'd probably be settled enough by then. And of course I could see her in the holidays.

By October we had about thirty five horses grazing our paddocks. Half of them belonged to Ness but the other half were from random people who'd heard on the grapevine that they could agist on our property. Ness was forever getting calls and bringing new horses down.

She and Mum hung out all the time and were talking about starting a business together around riding and lessons and horse stuff in general. The rides which she'd been doing every three weeks or so became more frequent and Charlie, Josh, Tessa, James and I found ourselves with part time jobs (yes, okay, we worked for our mothers!) helping get the horses tacked up and sometimes even going out on the rides.

I'd given up on the idea of Charlie being in love with James. They were friends and joked around but there were no gooey gazes or giggling so I figured that was that. Anyway, at first I was pleased because if they had started going out I would have had to see him even more than I did normally. Don't get me wrong, he was actually pretty nice, and the more I hung out with him the more his looks seemed to go from ugly to okay to actually kind of handsome, but he unsettled me. I didn't really understand him.

To begin with, we talked a bit, but not very much and only about things like the weather or the saddles needing a polish. It was just everyday stuff and he didn't seem to have much else to say to me. It wasn't because he was a shy person though. He laughed and joked with the others with no problems. He just seemed to go quiet around me. I figured maybe he still hated me, but that didn't account for the times I'd turn around suddenly, in the stables or on a ride, and he would just be there, watching me, closer than I expected.

As the weeks went on, though, I found myself hoping to run into him more and more. It wasn't because we had more to say to each other. In fact, it was the exact opposite. It was the quietness that was the intriguing thing about him.

I hadn't been calm — ever — my entire life. I was always the kid with jellybeans in her feet; the exact opposite of quiet. So when it was just him and me and the horses in the stables, and he didn't talk, this weird thing happened where it felt like I was under some sort of magnetic trance and naturally calmed down as well. We just worked together, polishing tack and cleaning out stalls and sorting out gear.

The whole thing made me surprisingly dizzy. I had no idea you could just *be* in a room with someone else. Samantha would have gone crazy. She was fifty words a second most of the time. But I got used to it. In fact, I was nearly addicted to it. After a few weeks I found myself hoping that I'd find James by himself when I went over so that we could work together without talking to each other.

But it's not often that people change completely overnight, and it's especially not true for me. Some days the new 'quiet Coco' stayed peaceful and serene. It was on the other days I just couldn't help myself.

We were getting ready for a ride one afternoon and I stuck my head outside to see who the customers were. It was a disappointing view. About eight young looking people were hanging around, taking stuff out of their cars and getting helmets on. And all of them looked like they'd walked straight out of a cheap 1990s sitcom, but not in a cool, retro, hip kind of way. The hair was wrong, the clothes were wrong, the, well, everything was wrong.

"You have got to see this." I put my head back in the door and made big rolled eyes at James. "We're riding with the cast of the Big Bang Theory!"

James turned around to look at me but he wasn't laughing. "What?" he said, like he didn't understand.

"I'm serious," I said. I was giggling with delight. "These people are like, nerds from Nerdville. Seriously, one of them looks like that guy from Napoleon Dynamite."

James tightened his mouth. And then he stood up. My eyes followed him to his full height. I felt vaguely nervous.

"They're people, Coco," he said. He looked disappointed and then he turned away.

"Can't I call someone a nerd?" I said. "Maybe it takes a nerd to know one." I giggled, but it was weak.

He stopped still for a minute and then he turned around and looked straight at me. His face seemed puzzled. I tried to keep a smile on my face but it only lasted a second. And then I felt small down in the pit of my stomach.

"I don't know why you do that, Coco," he said. "You don't need to be—I don't know—cooler than everybody the entire time. I like it when you're just being yourself." He turned around again and started buckling Boldy's girth.

That night I shifted and fidgeted under my doona. Why did it bother me so much what James thought? Why did it affect me so much when he made that disappointed face? And why did he have to be so straightforward? It was all too annoying. I decided that the next time I saw him, I'd just pretend everything was alright. It was easier that way. All of this figuring-stuff-out-with-blue-eyed-boys took way too much energy.

Anyway, I had something else to distract me.

The internet had come to Budgong.

I couldn't believe that I had lived for eight months without (a) Facebook, (b) email or (c) online chat. In the beginning I had felt like I was having email withdrawals. It got easier of course, but I was desperate to get on the net again and when Dad said one night that the phone company had been down to install some sort of connection thingy, I held in my excitement until he'd gone out of the shed. Then I literally bounced on my toes and listened to myself make some sort of unexplained and unexpected 'eeeee-eeeeee-eeeee' little-girl-style squealing noise.

It wasn't immediate, of course. What was, around here? We still had to wait a few weeks until the solar panels were installed so we could actually use the phone line connection. Or something. I didn't really get it. All I knew was that the first night that we actually had proper lights instead of kerosene lanterns we had a party. As the designated lantern cleaner I was especially celebratory. That was one less chore for me to wreck my nails on. The next day an electrician installed a plug that I could charge my laptop on and a connection for the net. True, it didn't work perfectly, but we had a few usable hours each day and I could check my email.

Which turned out to be chockers.

I had a bit of junk mail and some random messages from a few different school people, but mostly my inbox was crammed with messages from Samantha. Two hundred and eighty-seven of them to be exact. When I checked the dates, they were mostly written in the autumn, just after we'd moved. Then she'd obviously given up because there were only two in winter and a final message from about two months ago:

Hi Coco? Are you out there? Still no Internet connection? Couldn't you even drive into a town and check it at a library or a cafe or something? Have you fallen off the face of the earth? Are you dead? Are you ever coming back? Sam xxxxxooooooxxxxx

Outside it was a sunny spring day but I shivered. There was a feeling in my chest I couldn't quite name, even though it felt familiar. It was a mix between cold and ill and fear. *This is weird,* I said to myself. There was nothing specific in her email which made me uncomfortable. But I felt really off-beam. And it took me about three days before I was ready to write back.

Hey Sam.

Finally got internet on so I got your emails—eventually. Life has been... different. It seems like a long time ago that we were on the bus together. I told James—he's the boy next door—about you. He's mostly nice but his clothes are dodgy. I've been riding a horse called Cupcake. She's beautiful and kind of 'my own' horse. It's a long story. But you can tell the girls that I'm fine and school is strict and I'm not allowed any emails. I don't know. Make something up. Miss you.

Coco xxx

I don't know why, but I wasn't expecting to hear from her for a while. I think I had forgotten how instant emails are. So it was almost shocking when Samantha replied the same afternoon.

Hi Coco,

Omigosh! You're alive! Who knew? I'd given up—almost. Told the girls I heard from you. They texted Mr Perfect (yes,

Darcy—he's SO gorgeous) straight away cos he still wants to meet you. Can't wait til you get to meet him too. We can trade notes.

Are you coming back any time soon?

Life here is SO gorgeous. SO happy you went away (well, not really, but you understand, right?). It's SO great being friends with Saff and Ti. They're SO nice. And really cool. We understand each other heaps. Same sense of humour. I've been comforting Saff since she broke up with Ed. SO sad for him, but she's glad she dumped him.

Isabella copied Tiger by dying her hair and it looks terrible. She talks too much all the time but we just tell her to shut up. Can't wait till you get back and we'll be part of it all together. A year seems like SUCH a long time, right?

Love, Sammi (everyone calls me that now...)


I looked at her message and closed the computer and sat there for a moment. That weird thing inside was back. I felt confused. Or maybe hungry. Or something. I wasn't sure. It was uncomfortable, like someone was slowly tipping over my chair.

"You okay, sweetie?" Mum asked. She was watching me from the kitchen part of the shed.

"Yes. I guess." I shook myself. "Yes. I'm fine."

*No, I'm not,* I thought. *I'm not fine. But I don't know why.*

"I'm going out to see Cupcake." I grabbed my helmet and a halter. I'd sort out 'Sammi' and Darcy and Isabella and Tiger and Saffron and everything else later. Right now, a bareback ride would make me feel more like myself.

# CHAPTER 18

As the weather got warmer, more people were booking rides on the weekend and Mum and Ness's business was taking off.

James and I were back to being mostly friends again, riding together almost every day and working together some weekends. I kept my comments about other people to myself and pretended everything was okay between us and it seemed to work. In fact, we were probably getting on better than before, which was weird. He now smiled when I said something funny (which was pretty frequent because I can be amusing when I try, and I was trying pretty hard because I definitely preferred it when he was friends with me). If his eyes were his best feature, his smile was definitely his second best.

In late Spring Ness called me to ask if I'd help one Saturday afternoon.

"It's a bigger group than normal," she said. "A whole extended family thing. The people are from Sydney and they want to go out for three hours."

Ness paid good rates and I wanted the money so I said yes. Josh and Charlie had other things to do so I ended up working with just Ness, James and Tessa.

The group was celebrating a sixtieth birthday and I was guessing the birthday girl was the mother of the family because she was smiling widely and bossing everyone else around.

"I love riding and I hate parties," she said loudly to Ness, who smiled patiently. "So I decided that at the age of sixty I could do what I wanted. No party! Instead, I'm making all my family ride with me. I've roped them all in and they can't get away!"

The family were classy. Even if I'd wanted to laugh at them, there would have been nothing to pick on. They dressed well, they looked expensive and the younger ones appeared bored in a cool way. *Kind of like Saffron and Tiger*, I thought, and a tiny blob of jealousy started to bubble up in my brain. I was supposed to be saddling up but I couldn't stop looking at them. There were about five or six boys and girls about my age or a bit older standing at the back of the group waiting to be fitted for helmets. I took a deep breath and remembered I was supposed to be working. *Stop getting distracted*, I thought.

But that was before I saw him.

The. Most. Incredibly. Handsome. Boy.

Ever.

He was surrounded by the others but as the group thinned out, there he appeared like a rainbow in the sky. Yes, I know it's a cliché but I'll admit to another one as well. It's slightly embarrassing, but the second my eyes found him, my heart made a tiny little noise which could really only be described as 'pitter patter'.

I lost my grip on the saddle I was throwing over Boldy

and it went too far and landed on the ground on the other side. Boldy pulled back in fright.

"Sorry, boy," I said. "Sorry." But I wasn't really trying to calm him down. My eyes were still locked on Mr Gorgeous.

A tiny bell went off in my brain. For some reason he looked familiar. I ran through all the possibilities — was he a brother or cousin of one of my friends? An acquaintance of an acquaintance? It was odd, but I couldn't figure it out and in the end I had to conclude I'd never met him before. But it didn't matter. I couldn't stop looking at his dark eyes, dark hair, muscles and a jaw line to die for. I melted slightly into my boots.

It was at that point I realised I was wearing very ugly boots. As well as dirty jodhpurs and a flanny.

*Great.* So much for thinking it wouldn't matter what I wore just because I was riding.

I tried to hide behind Boldy so the boy could only see my head. At least I had some mascara and eyeliner on. I could hear his mother worrying at him: "Dee, do you have the right kind of jeans on? Can you make sure the others all put on their helmets?"

"Yes, Mum, take it easy." He patted her on the back to reassure her but when she turned away he made a rude face. I laughed inside. If Ness saw that she'd have something to say. Once Tessa had done the same thing to her and she got a dressing down like I'd never seen from Ness.

"You don't get to treat me like that, young lady," she'd said. "I don't mind if you tell me what's on your mind. I don't mind if you're angry with me. But you say what you think. Let it out. You don't walk away and pretend and then blow me off like that. It's not honest. It doesn't work for anyone in real life and it's not going to work here."

Dee had gone back to talking with the others. They were circled around him, giggling while he talked. The three girls were all trying their best to give him big-eyed looks and at one point he reached out to one of them and circled her in a hug.

*Too bad,* I said to myself. *He's got a girl...* but I couldn't finish my thought. James tapped me on the shoulder.

"Are you actually going to put that saddle on?" he said. "Do you want me to fix it? What are you doing?" He turned to see what I was looking at, narrowed his eyes and then turned back to me.

I hadn't thought my tongue was hanging out, but he must have seen something that said 'puppy crush' and from his look I could see something was wrong. I tried to fix up my face to look disinterested and neutral but it was too late.

"Really, Coco? Are you for real?" he said. He sounded disappointed. Bored even. He turned away to pick up the saddle.

I was annoyed. "So what? I'm just admiring a pretty face. Haven't you ever done that?"

"He might be pretty, but you can tell straight away he's not a good guy," he said. "Look. It's all about him. He's not interested in anyone else."

"What are you talking about?" I said. I looked around. Dee had his arm around one of the other girls now. "He's cool, that's all. Cool people don't have to be interested in anyone else. Anyway, they probably are—it's just they don't need to show it. That's why they're cool." I was getting confused. "I mean, it doesn't matter." I teased him. "Maybe you're just jealous."

"Jealous?" said James. "What would I be jealous of?"

"Maybe that he's getting some admiration?" I said. I made a face. "Look at Tessa."

If I'd been gooey-eyed, Tessa was in full on puppy-love mode. Josh was forgotten. Dee was the 'it' boy. She was sorting out his horse and trying to get noticed. Unfortunately, when he did notice her, it was because of her, ahem, chest. I saw his eyes go from her bust to her face to her bust again. And then he smiled.

James' eyes narrowed. "That guy had better watch it," was all he said. I gave him a look.

"What are you going to do? Arrest him?" I said. "Have you got your handcuffs? Do you keep them in your hat?"

But James walked away without answering and my teasing words fluttered into the empty breeze and then plopped down into a puddle of mud and horse poo all mixed together. I rolled my eyes at him for good measure and said *Humph* under my breath because sometimes that just helps when you feel a little bit embarrassed.

The ride started. I was on Cupcake, who was great except when she saw a kangaroo in the distance. "Steady," I said. "Calm down. Keep walking."

Ness laughed. "She really doesn't like them. And she hates wombats. You'll have to watch out she doesn't get spooked one day. If you go out in the evening, that is."

I was watching out, but it wasn't for Cupcake. It was for Dee. I kept my eyes on him, laughing and joking with his friends, the whole time. And on Tessa, who was following along behind, more in love than I'd ever seen anyone.

We wound around the path, up the fire trails, through the creek and into rain forest. Then it was up the cliff face where we stood to admire the view. Half way through we came down again and to the edge of the dam, in a paddock with a wooded bush area to one side.

"We'll let the horses take a drink," said Ness and everyone got off. "And we can have some refreshments too." She got a surprisingly un-squashed cake and a knife out of a saddle bag, cut it up and handed it around. "Happy Birthday, Martine".

"Oh, thank you!" the mother gushed. "Oh, this is so lovely! I'm so glad I didn't have a party. This is just beautiful," and she went around kissing and double kissing everyone on the cheek while they all said, 'Cheers,' and, 'Congratulations,' and held up plastic glasses filled from water bottles to toast her.

It was then, in the middle of the noise and happy-birthday-hubbub that I needed to go to the bathroom. We were still a good hour from home and I knew I couldn't wait that long so I slipped into the bush area away from the group to find a good spot. I was fussy about where I went after the whole slip-and-fall-mud-and-leech episode so I was looking around carefully for a place that was sheltered but not wet, as well as undetectable but not impossible to get into, when I saw someone ahead of me. And some voices. Through the trees, I could see a flash of red, the same colour as Tessa's t-shirt. And then I could hear the voices get louder, almost urgent.

And then it sounded like one of the voices was upset, and saying, 'No,' so I pushed through some dead tree branches to see.

It was Tessa, in her red t-shirt of course. But who was she with? I couldn't quite make it out, although it looked like a boy and it looked like he had dark hair, but he was standing so close, almost pushing her over that I couldn't quite tell. *Is it Dee?* I thought. *Are they... kissing?* But Tessa was kind of pushing him away for some reason.

I didn't want to disturb her, but it didn't look right.

"Hey, excuse me," I said. "Um, sorry."

As the boy looked up I could see it definitely was Dee. But Tessa didn't look like she was in love any more. As soon as he moved she tore herself away from him and ran away crying, leaving me face to face with Dee.

An hour before I would have been ecstatic and excited to be alone with him. And don't get me wrong, he was still gorgeous. But now it felt different. I saw a flash of anger in his eyes.

"Sorry, just looking for a place to go to the loo," I said awkwardly, backing away.

He looked at me scornfully up and down and then stepped heavily past me without talking.

I stood there for a good minute, confused and almost a bit shell shocked. *Should I check on Tessa?* I thought. *This is so weird.* I scrabbled out past shrubs and dead trees and came out to the group who were still eating and chatting. Tessa was nowhere to be seen, so I looked around for James.

"Hey, have you seen Tessa? This funny thing happened," I said. "I don't mean funny-ha-ha."

He raised his eyebrows. "What?"

"She was in that bit of the bush, just like a minute ago with that guy Dee and she looked really upset."

He turned his head, looking for her. "What happened?"

"Well I don't know. I mean, he looked kind of, well, angry. And she ran off crying. So..." It was hard to explain. Plus I felt super-embarrassed describing what I saw. "I just think you'd better see if she's okay."

James' face looked black. "I'm going to get that guy."

"What? No," I said. "Check that Tessa's okay. I'd find her but I'm desperate to go, you know..." and I gestured towards the bush and jumped up and down a little bit so he got the message.

When I came back, thankfully with no leeches on my bottom (or at least, none that I knew about) I found Tessa standing off to the side next to Boldy, quiet and angry and shaking her head. James was talking to her. He looked alarmed.

"Just tell me what happened."

"No, it was nothing," she was saying. "Just leave it, James. Not here. I'm okay."

"If he hurt you..." He looked around accusingly at the group of people still milling around, admiring the view. Martine was at the centre of everything, monopolizing Ness and hanging off her arm. "Tell me all about this amazing property," she was saying. I could see Dee on the other side of the group standing with his friends again, laughing and joking. But I could tell that he wasn't really back to normal. He kept shooting death glances over to James and Tessa for some reason.

On the ride back Tessa and James and I stayed together

at the back. Tessa was quiet. I was confused. James was angry. And I mean really angry.

When we got to the stables he waited until they were all about to leave and then he pulled Dee aside at the last minute.

"Watch it, mate." He had his hand on his shoulder. I noticed that James was taller.

Dee shook him off. "Hey, you don't touch the shirt." Then he looked at James' flanny shirt and his old jeans and laughed up close to his face. But it was more of a smirk. "Don't touch what you can't afford, mate."

"I know your type," said James. He hadn't moved. Instead, he just seemed to get bigger.

But Dee could match him. "None of your business, mate," he said. "Stay cool." And he shrugged loosely. Then he got in his new model BMW with his laughing friends and was driven away.

It took another half hour to un-tack the horses and put everything away. Ness left us to it. I don't think she'd realised anything was wrong and after ten minutes Tessa said, "I've got a headache," and went home too. James and I worked in silence as usual but this time it was like walking on sharp knives.

When I finally couldn't stand it anymore, I blurted out, "So what actually happened? Did Tessa tell you?"

"I can't tell you," said James. He had his back to me, hanging up the tack. "She doesn't want to talk about it. She doesn't want anyone to know." But then, a second later, he turned around. His eyes were burning blue.

"I know you liked him, Coco. But you should stay away from guys like that. I know what they're like. I've lived through the hassles they cause. Really. You should stay away."

"But why?" I said. "Did he and Tessa have an argument or something? Why were they even in the bushes?"

"Are you really so naive?" said James. He looked at me like he was just seeing me for the first time. "He's a creep. He was being creepy," he said, his eyebrows furrowed, but not with anger. It was more like he was trying to kindly explain something to me. "Do you get it?"

"But I don't understand..." I said. "He looked... I don't know... nice. He looked cool."

James made that noise that people make when they're annoyed and they kind of breathe out through their nose but really sharp. *Shmhhhhn.*

"Yeah. He *looked* cool," he said. He took a breath and then let it out again, like he'd thought about saying something else but then decided not to keep talking. "You know what? I'm done. I'm going home."

I saw him shrug his shoulders and shake his head as walked across the driveway and up the path to his house. I looked after him, confused. *Really? Creepy? That's so weird.*

# CHAPTER 19

You'd think by this time I would have had enough changes in my life. You'd think that I would have deserved just a little bit of peace, a little bit of space, a little bit of tranquillity.

You'd think.

Ha.

Something was about to happen that would change everything, all over again. And just like before, I had no idea it was coming.

After the Tessa/Dee incident I decided to again try my tactic of pretending everything was okay between James and me but I didn't really even have to because I hardly saw him at all. It wasn't because he was avoiding me, or because we weren't getting along. The main reason was that our house was actually, finally getting built.

The walls were going up and everyone was getting roped in to help.

It was a messy business. Dad wasn't kidding around when he'd first mentioned mud brick. He actually meant bricks made out of mud. So we made mud bricks. And then we put them together into walls of mud bricks. And then we covered the whole thing with more mud.

At the same time we covered ourselves with mud.

No one got a break. Every single one of us ended up brown and mucky, head to toe, every single day. It was disgusting. But there was no getting out of it. Dad was a surprisingly hard taskmaster. At first I complained and whinged and was kind of grossed out but honestly, once you're covered with mud, it really doesn't matter if you get a bit more on you. Somewhere around the third week it became normal. Plus as the walls got higher I actually got excited. The house was a good design and I liked to walk around on the slab floor and picture where my room would be.

But at the end of the day, every day, I was a mess.

The new solar panels were heating up water which was nice. We didn't have to boil drums of water for hours like before, but now the length of our showers were strictly policed by Dad who had some kind of outside control built in.

"Coco! One more minute," he'd yell, "and then I'm turning off the hot water." A couple of times I stayed in too long and got completely frozen when he got sick of waiting for me. The shower was never long enough for me to really get my hair clean and it was a sad day when I realised that I'd said a permanent goodbye to shiny. Now my hair was pretty much stiff all the time. It looked like it had that really expensive product in it that boys use to get that 'bed hair' look. In fact, Josh's hair looked awesome most of the time. But I'm not big on bed hair and the whole mud-as-a-stylist-product thing wasn't really doing it for me.

A couple of times Samantha emailed me and suggested we chat on Skype but I put her off. I didn't want her to see how I was looking. I could hear the criticism in her voice without even talking to her. So I just said that there wasn't enough reception on our dodgy internet, that the video link didn't work properly and the audio was scratchy.

But secretly, I was starting to not care so much about how I looked, especially when we were working. I dressed up to go out, of course, like I always had, but I wasn't that fussed when no one else except family could see me. It kind of felt comfortable. And when we were all muddy, and all working, it was actually pretty fun, even though I didn't really want to admit it.

The other thing I didn't want to admit was that I was confused about Dad.

By this time, I hadn't actually spoken to him for months, not since my birthday. We'd developed a sort of habit of communicating via Mum (although she still didn't like it) but I think Dad was seeing if he could outlast me. Before, he would have either yelled at me or he would have begged me to talk and offered gifts until I did. Now, it looked like he was determined to do some sort of new parenting thing and wait me out.

So it was up to me.

At the beginning I'd said I wasn't going to talk to him for a year. But a year was starting to feel kind of long. On the other hand, even though I was feeling happier, I still felt cross that he had moved us. If we hadn't come here I wouldn't have been feeling bad to begin with, so it wasn't as if he had actually done anything good, right?

And I was still very much planning to go back to Sydney.

The reason I was even thinking about it was because I nearly forgot the whole no-talking thing one day. We were lifting bricks and he said something as simple as, "Watch out Coco. Don't want to fall backwards," and up into my mouth came the words, "It's okay, Dad," and then I suddenly remembered that I wasn't talking to him and shut my mouth so they didn't come out but I looked at him and he looked at me and really the words were completely beside the point because we'd communicated anyway. And I couldn't tell him so but the look we had felt warm and familiar. And I realised I'd missed him. A lot.

And then I didn't know what to do. But I thought I'd better stick to my word and see the year through, even though I didn't really want to anymore. I still had to show Dad that he couldn't push me around because I was still angry about it even though I was a bit happier.

I know. It sounds complicated. My head hurt when I thought about it.

Sometimes when Dad was building he got Mum to go into Kangaroo Valley to the post office or to pick something up from the little hardware-shop-that-was-not-a-hardware-shop. This shop sold everything: hardware, fishing tackle, chickens and, get this, antiques. (Seriously, country businesses make me laugh. Does someone just wake up one morning and say, "I know what I want to do with the rest of my life. I'd like to open a shop that sells building supplies, poultry and vintage goods. Oh, and I'll cater for the local fisher folk as well"?)

If we decided to go with her, Mum would usually

buy us a hot chocolate at a little cafe without a name (the owner turned out to be a woman called Charlie which our Charlie liked a lot, plus she made the milk really fluffy and always added a marshmallow). Other times we'd get to look in the shops which turned out to be kind of cute. I mean, I'm not into rocking horses or wooden bowls but there were some earrings even I would have worn in one of the gift shops. And Charlie can never walk past homemade fudge.

I didn't realise that it would be in the sleepy little village of Kangaroo Valley that everything would change all over again for me.

The day that it all started turned out to be a normal Spring day. Charlie, Josh and I had been working with Dad on the house all morning and Mum had been working with Ness. Suddenly she came tearing across the paddock. "I've got to go get some horse feed and this is the only time I can do it: do you want to come?"

It's weird how one decision—one tiny little decision that hardly even seems important—can have everything to do with your future. I didn't know that this trip was going to have bigger consequences than I could imagine. I couldn't have known that my dreams and hopes were going to be tossed around again without me even being aware of it.

"Yes or no. Right now," said Mum.

"Yes, okay," I said, shrugging, and climbed in the car with Charlie.

It was only then that I looked at her and she looked at me and we both said, "Yuck!" Our hair was muddy, our clothes were caked and our gumboots could hardly be seen because of the layer of brown all over them. Even Charlie's face had brown splatters on it.

But it was such a beautiful day that I was more interested in enjoying the sunshine than looking at myself. Anyway, no one knew me in Kangaroo Valley, so how could it matter if anyone saw me?

We dropped into the hardware shop and put the mortar and the horse stuff in the bag. "Hey, Charlie, look," I giggled. "You could buy eggs and paint."

"Yeah," she said. "Or screwdrivers and a vintage chair."

"Stop it, you two," said Mum. "The man will hear you. You're being rude." She got out her credit card and went to pay. "I think we should probably go straight home," she said in-between pressing buttons on the machine. "Dad will be expecting us back and Ness needs the feed this afternoon."

"Noooo," whined Charlie, like a five year old. "Can't we get a drink? Please? Pretty please?"

I added my voice to hers. "Go on Mum. It's like the first time we've seen actual buildings and people for weeks. I think my body is saying that I neeed a hot chocolate too."

Mum clicked her tongue against her teeth and gave us a look. "Okay. But just a quick one. We've got to get going."

Later, when I thought about it, I realised that if we'd gone back to the farm, everything would have been different. I never would have been seen and the photo would never have been taken. But how can you know the future? And would you want to, even if you could?

We sat in the cafe waiting for our drinks and watching

the tourists go by. For such a little town the place was packed. There were bikie couples in black leather, caravan tourists in shorts and joggers, lovey-dovey weekend-away couples and family groups with kids and teenagers.

With sunshine on my back, fresh air in my nostrils and warm hot chocolate in my mouth I couldn't help smiling inside, even though I didn't want to let it be known that I thought Kangaroo Valley was actually one of the cutest places I'd ever seen.

"This is such a gorgeous place," said Charlie.

"I know," said Mum. "I love it."

"It's pretty good," I said. "I mean, it's not Sydney, but there are some cute shops. And it's pretty."

Mum looked at me, pleased. "I'm so glad you're feeling more at home here."

"A bit. Not completely," I said, although I knew I was fibbing. "You know I'm going back to Sydney next year still, right?"

"Yes, yes, yes," she said, still smiling. "Although I wonder how you'll feel about that after Pony Camp. I have this feeling it's going to change things for you."

"Change? Maybe not. But it'll be an awesome weekend," I said. "I'm looking forward to it.

The talk about Pony Camp had been building for months. My attitude had gone from don't-care-a-single-bit to vaguely-but-not-openly-curious to can't-wait-till-it's-on. Ness had been running it for years and from everything Tessa and James said about it—the riding, the laughing, the staying up all night telling jokes—I was expecting a very fun weekend. Mum was going to help out with the cooking and looking after equipment but she'd promised to stay in the background so we wouldn't get embarrassed.

"It'll be great," said Mum. She swirled her coffee around in the cup and drank it down in one gulp. "Are you girls ready to go?"

"Do you mind if I just go over to the gift shop and see if they still have those earrings I was looking at last time?" I said. "I've got the money in my wallet today. I might buy them. But I'll be really quick."

"I'll come too," said Charlie but as she stood up she spilt the rest of her drink. "Whoops," she said, grabbing a napkin and dabbing at her T-shirt. "You go ahead. Don't worry about me. I'll be there in a sec."

So I headed across the road and into the shop. As I went in, I vaguely heard a gasp and the click of a camera but when I turned around to see what it was, the door of the shop swung shut onto my face. I rubbed my nose and blinked a few times and moved away from the door just in time to see Charlie come in, looking puzzled.

"I think someone just took your picture," she said.

"Who?" I said.

"I don't know. A girl. I've never seen her before. She was sitting in a cafe and I saw her watch you cross the road."

"Not Tessa?" She was the only girl that I knew here that I could think of.

"No, duh. Of course not Tessa. I think I could recognise her. This one had sunnies on. Kind of trendy. Red hair. A bit snooty maybe?"

"Creepy," I said. "Maybe it was a stalker." I made a

fake scaredy-cat face. "Or maybe not." My eyes lit up. "Maybe she's a model talent scout on holiday in sleepy Kangaroo Valley and she's just seen me cross the road and suddenly her holidays are over because she thinks I'm super gorgeous and she's going to call me up and offer me a contract to go to New York and Paris."

"You think?" Charlie looked towards my mud-spattered outfit. "Maybe in a parallel universe where dirty is clean and clean is dirty."

"Hmm. You're right. A shower is probably the first step towards a modelling contract in my case," I said, looking rueful.

"Yeah, but not with Dad timing you." Charlie laughed. "You've got to actually wash that hair you know."

The door swung open again, narrowly missing my nose. It was Mum. "Are you girls done yet? We really have to go."

With the trip home and the new earrings and the talk of Pony Camp, I forgot all about the stalker/model contract photograph thing. It hardly seemed important.

And anyway, something else happened the very next day. I got into an argument. And this one was a big one.

# CHAPTER 20

We were a week away from Pony Camp and all of us—Josh, Charlie, James, Tessa and me—had been pressed into service, despite the house building. Mud bricks could wait. The horses had to come first for a week and our job was to clean up the building behind the stables on Ness's property to make sure it was ready for when the campers arrived.

"It's where we'll sleep," explained Tessa, excitedly. She was finally coming back to her old happy self after the whole Dee incident. She'd gone quiet and miserable for a bit but it all seemed to be okay again now. "Basically, we hang out here when we're not riding."

"Which isn't much really," said James. "Most of the day we're on the horses. It's only at night and meals and things."

"Does everyone sleep in the same room?" asked Josh.

"No, silly," said Tessa. She smiled at him. It looked like it was on again between them. "It's girls on this side and boys over there." She pointed in the direction of two crowded bunk rooms, each on the end of the long main area. I looked around and wrinkled up my nose.

"It's kind of smelly," I said and I saw a tiny smile creep onto James' face.

"I think that's what the detergent and mops are for," said Charlie. She emptied her bucket of water on the floor and passed me the mop. "Come on, sunshine."

"Tell me you don't clean on Pony Camp," I said. "What else happens apart from riding?"

"If it's cool, we light a fire in the fireplace and usually Mum has marshmallows—like heaps of them—to toast," said Tessa.

"Yes, and then sometimes we play card games," said James. "Really late. I think last year we stayed up till about three am." He grinned at me.

"Doesn't Ness make you go to sleep?" Charlie asked.

"Ha ha, that's funny," said James. "If there are cards involved, she's up later than anyone. But normally she can only do it on the first night. The second night she's in bed by nine and snoring by ten." He grinned at me. I raised my eyebrows, amused.

"And last year, after she went to bed we played this massive game of Truth or Dare," said Tessa, her eyes shining. "It was so awesome—one guy actually climbed the roof of the stables and howled at the moon at midnight."

"That's cool!" said Josh.

"Awesome," said Charlie.

I was inspired. "Hey, we should play Truth or Dare right now." I looked at James who was still looking at me. "If we have to mop and clean at least we should do something interesting while we do it. What do you reckon?"

"Yeah, okay." James nodded. There was a twinkle in his eyes. "I'm in."

"So." I leant on my mop and tilted my head at him. "Truth or dare?"

"Hang on a minute," he said. "Not so fast. What are your rules?"

"Normal rules," I said. "Simple. You answer the question with the complete truth, no exceptions. Or else you accept the dare."

"What kind of questions are you going to ask?" I couldn't tell if he was teasing me or being straightforward.

"What do you mean? The usual kind, of course. Who do you like? Who do you fancy? That kind of stuff." I looked at him, my eyes big with pretend exasperation. "You're just trying to stall. What will it be? Truth? Or dare?" I tipped my head on the side, daring him with my voice.

His blue eyes caught the light and he hesitated for a second, but I couldn't read his expression.

"I'll take a dare," he said.

"Alright," whooped Josh. "It's on."

The four of us had to come up with a dare for James. Which was harder said than done. He was pretty much immune to the smell of horse poo and none of us could have stomached seeing him eat it so we let that idea slide. He could ride anything anywhere so a bareback gallop down the paddock was too easy. I was for suggesting that he climb up the inside of the chimney but Tessa reminded us that we'd be just making more soot and mess for ourselves to clean up. Finally Josh looked up and around at the millions of daddy longlegs spiders on the wall and ceiling.

"Why don't we make it that he has to eat a spider?" he said.

"Three spiders," said Tessa, jumping up and down.

"No, five," I said, giving him a look. "Five squishy, crunchy spiders. Yummy yummy."

It took a little while to catch the spiders but pretty soon James had them all in his mouth. "Delicious," he said, and he opened his mouth and stuck out his tongue to show us that they'd gone down. "Ahh."

"Ew," I said, shuddering, but I was giggling too. "I can't believe you did that."

"Just like chicken," he said, teasing me. "You should try some."

Next we dared Josh to climb on the roof, which he did with a few wobbles and a few tiny flashes of fear in his eyes that probably only Charlie and I saw. Tessa seemed appropriately impressed. And then we asked Charlie who she liked for her truth question, but it was a very disappointing answer.

"No one." She grinned. "I'm serious. I don't like anyone. That's the absolute truth."

"That's not fair," I said. "No fun. You should do another one."

"No way," she said. "It's your fault for not asking a better question."

It was Tessa's turn next and, like Charlie, she chose truth.

"Don't waste the question," I said to the others before anyone could speak. "Seriously. We probably already know who she likes." At this Tessa went red and Josh lowered his eyes. "We should ask a different question. Make it worthwhile."

Everyone started to think. Should it be about horses? School? Old crushes? Suddenly I knew what to ask. It was perfect.

"I've got it! Don't say anything, anyone!" I said quickly. "Tessa, here's your question. Which is your ugliest feature? Your face, your bust or your dress sense?"

I told you earlier that I had a tendency to shoot off my mouth without thinking.

In my brain, it had all sounded so clever. Funny. Ironic, even. But as soon as the words came out of my mouth and met the open air, I saw them turn into tiny pieces of sharp glass and whiz through the room like bullets. I could see Tessa wincing, physically injured by each one as it came at her.

I stood for a second, aghast at what I'd done. And then the room turned into one of those ads where everyone stops except for the main character and the world is kind of frozen in one moment.

But then it unfroze. And the repercussions began.

First Tessa gasped at me. She was open mouthed. She swallowed, went to speak, swallowed and looked at me. "I, um," she said. And then she couldn't say anything at all. Instead, she turned and ran.

The door slammed and Charlie was at me.

"Coco. I can't believe you said that. What were you thinking?"

"Good one, dumb-brain," came Josh's voice from behind. "Look what you've done. How do you think you're going to slide out of making the insult of the century?"

I was waiting for James's voice, but he had nothing to say. He just turned away, but not before I caught a glimpse of his face. It was disappointed and sad. I dropped my mop on the floor with a splash.

And then I turned and ran in the opposite direction. All the way back to the farm.

# CHAPTER 21

My face was flushed when I reached the shed and it wasn't just from running. I shot past Dad, ignored Mum and flung myself straight onto my bed. My chest was heaving and I nearly felt like throwing up. It wasn't fair. I hadn't meant to upset Tessa. They had no right to get so mad at me about it. It was just a game. And everyone knows that when you go for truth in Truth and Dare you have to take whatever questions come to you. Anyway, it wasn't as if Tessa thought she was perfect looking. She asked me to help her with her makeup all the time, and only a few weeks ago when we were looking through a magazine we found a section on dressing for your figure shape and she herself had pointed out the tips to minimise her chest, so it wasn't as if she didn't know she was big.

But I still couldn't shake the feeling that I'd done something terrible. Especially when I thought about the look on James's face.

Why were his eyes so blue? Why did I care what he thought? And why did he look so disappointed in me so often?

I made a growl of frustration and slammed the doona with my fist. If only these people weren't my friends. If only I was back in Sydney with people who understood me. Samantha would never get offended by a question like that. In fact, she'd probably be the one asking it about me. Country people could never take a joke. And now I'd either have to apologise or go to Pony Camp with everybody mad at me.

I rolled my eyes—a full roll—around and around. *I am so sick of this place,* I thought. *I just have to get out of here.*

An actual escape was impossible, but when my eyes finally came to rest on my laptop I decided a virtual escape would have to do. At least for now, anyway. I flipped it open, connected the internet and checked my email.

There, in my inbox, was my saviour. It was an email from Samantha. And it solved two problems in one.

Coco! Really important! Saff is having a party this weekend. Really big deal, heaps of boys, lots of cool people. Ti and everyone will be there. Even better: it's at her house in Vaucluse right on the harbour. She says that you'll be finished at your 'school' (she looked up the term dates on the school website) so she reckons there's no reason you can't come. Told me to invite you.

Seriously Coco, you have to make it. This is a big one. They're starting to ask why you aren't back yet. You've got to make an appearance, or maybe they won't have you back next year.

Sam

PS. Darcy is going to be there. And believe me, he's heaps

better looking in real life. He said last time he wants to see you—he doesn't believe you're real.

My heart jumped. First with excitement, second with relief and third with fear. And then it did an extra little hop, skip and jump for another reason altogether: Darcy.

This would be the answer to my problems. I could skip Pony Camp altogether, avoid having to apologise to Tessa, get to catch up with my Sydney friends, re-cement my place in the group and meet my dream boy Darcy all in one night. One look at him and James' blue eyes would be out of my head for ever. And then by the time I got back, the fight would have blown over and we could all have a happy summer holiday before I left to go back to Sydney in the new school year.

Yes, this was definitely a plan that could work.

My stomach was nervous though. Would the girls still like me? Would I be able to keep the story going about the school? Would I still fit in like I had before? And, most importantly, would Darcy like me?

The shed door slammed and I heard Charlie's boots stomp across the floor.

"Coco? Are you here? Are you okay?" She sounded concerned.

"I'm on my bed," I said. I didn't want to say any more.

"I know you didn't mean it about Tessa," she said. She sat down next to me. "But she is really upset. You'd probably better apologise, especially before Pony Camp."

I rolled away from her. "Maybe I did mean it. Anyway, I'm not going to go to Pony Camp." I pointed to the screen of the laptop. "I've been invited to a party.

It sounds like more fun."

Charlie read through the email. As soon as she saw Samantha's name she rolled her eyes. "Pfft. That girl? Seriously, why would you want to go to a party with her when you can go to Pony Camp? You don't want to miss out on the social occasion of the year, do you? You're always wanting friends. This is the place to make them."

"*This* is the social occasion of the year!" I pointed to my computer screen, angry. "*These* are my friends. Those other people — Tessa, James and all the other horse-loving bumpkins — are just fill-ins for me. I'm not planning to stay here, you know. Mum promised I could go back to Sydney and I'm going to. I can go to Pony Camp any time. Anyway, I wouldn't even like anyone who goes there."

"How do you know you don't like them? You haven't even met them." Charlie sounded shocked.

"I already know, okay? Anyway, it's compared to the other people. I like Sydney people better. I just do. It's how I am. I've fitted in here because I've had to and because there's been no one else, but you know I'm not meant to be here. I'm a different person to you." I sat up and shook out my hair.

Charlie sat up next to me and imitated my hair shake, but in a mean way. "Yeah, you're different because you're a snob. You're just someone who thinks she's better than everyone else."

"That's not true." I was hurt. "I don't think I'm better than everybody else."

"Well how come even before today you still hardly talked to Tessa?"

"I talked to her." I shrugged.

"Yeah, but only ever to tell her she's wearing the wrong thing. You're basically mean, Coco. You think you're helping her but you're actually only hurting her feelings. And she's been really upset, especially since that guy did all that gross stuff to her on that ride you guys went on."

"What?"

"Didn't you even know? That's how much you even care about her. That guy Dee, the good looking, creepy one took her into the bush and tried to kiss her and touch her and all kinds of stuff."

"Eeewww." I put my hands over my ears. "He can't have."

"Why not?" said Charlie.

"Well, he looked so nice," I said.

"Well, he's not. He said some really horrible things to her and she felt so bad, like it was her fault. If James hadn't managed to get her to tell him, he might have got away with it," she said. "Or done something worse. Anyway, that's so typical of you. As soon as someone's pretty or good looking or wears good clothes you think they're perfect. But if someone looks like, I don't know... normal or a bit funny or even ugly, you don't even treat them like a person."

"I do too," I said. "It's just when they won't even try, I can't help it. I just don't like people who look like..."

"... like Tessa?" said Charlie. Her voice was getting louder. "She is who she is. She wears the wrong shirts for her shape. But it's not a crime. It's not..." she searched for the word, "... evil. You treat her like she's done something actually wrong. I can't tell you how many times I've had to apologise for you to her. You're lucky she still even talks to you. I don't know what your problem is."

"Whatever," I said. I made a face at her. "Anyway, it's not my fault she's shy and takes things personally. I can't help it if she doesn't want to hear the truth."

"You can talk." She sounded huffy.

"What does that mean?" Now I was angry. My voice was loud.

"You're the one who doesn't want to hear the real truth."

"Oh, and what's the real truth, Miss Smartypants?" I was trying to stop from yelling. I didn't want Mum to hear us.

"Basically you're rude, you're up yourself and you think you're better than everyone. Tessa puts up with you because of me and Josh. And James doesn't have any time for you."

I went cold. How dare Charlie talk to me about James. He was none of her business.

"Forget Pony Camp. There's no way I'm going, even if Mum won't let me go to the party. I'd prefer to stay here." I turned away from her and stalked stiffly through the kitchen and right out of the shed. If I could have slammed the door, I would have. I went straight down to Cupcake who was standing by the fence, eating grass. Her life was so simple. No parties, no dream crushes and no twin sisters to tell her things she didn't want to hear.

"I don't care if it's true," I told her. "I'm not going. I'm going to Sydney and I'm going to see all my actual friends again. The people I like and who like me."

Cupcake nibbled my hand and I gave her a carrot and a scratch. She nuzzled into me and her big eyes said, 'I get it. Poor, poor Coco.'

"What would I do without you, sweet horse?" I whispered. "You're my best friend."

# CHAPTER 22

Charlie was still mad at me three days later. She would hardly look at me and her answers to my deliberately polite questions were snippy and short. For myself, I had decided to put the fight behind me. If she wanted to be unforgiving, that was her problem. The fact was, I had something much more important on my mind: how to convince Mum to let me go to Saffron's party.

For three whole days I gave it my best shot and used every trick in my repertoire. And yes, there are a few different methods I know. I list them here in case someone ever needs them.

*Coco's definitive list to getting her own way.*

Hoping: always try this first. If you can get what you want from simply mentioning it in a positive, hopeful tone of voice, you can save a lot of energy.

Being nice: doing helpful things, giving back rubs and generally being pleasant to be around can work wonders. Watch for the happy surprised look to come across their faces and then move in with your request.

Writing convincing letters: if you can show parents all the reasons why they should let you do it and write down effective rebuttals to the reasons why you know they won't let you do it, they'll be so impressed at your initiative, education and maturity that they just might say yes anyway.

Pleading: when positive approaches don't work, you move on to pleading. This is best done with a plaintive voice and lots of long 'pleases'. Big eyes are essential but you have to be careful not to bat eyelashes otherwise it looks like obvious manipulation.

Sobbing: ranges from a subtle, choked up voice through to outright blubbering. Crying real tears if you can possibly swing it looks more realistic.

Begging: along the same lines as pleading but it has to come from a helpless, hopeless, pathetic mindset.

Threatening: you have to be careful not to go too far as it may backfire badly, but hinting about how miserable you can make someone else's life if you don't get what you want can really be effective.

Bluffing: the next step along from threatening. You have to be convincing and definite about the fact that you really can carry out the threat you've made.

Mum ignored my hopeful mentions and looked doubtful when I suggested that she sit down and let me wash up for her. When I brought out my page full of arguments as to why I should go, she said, "Could I please read this later? I'm very tired tonight." She endured two days of pleading and begging and just before I hit threatening and bluff she said these words: "Okay, Coco. You can go – if you ask your father."

"What?" I spluttered. "Really?"

"Yes," she said. She had an annoyingly superior smile

on her face. "You'll actually have to look in his face, use words, ask him a question and then listen for the answer. Do all of this without rudeness or rolling your eyes and you can go."

"Okay," I said, very careful to keep my eyes perfectly still. "Okay. Thanks, Mum."

I walked down the end of the paddock. Dad was up at the house site. I was torn. And confused. It was a bit like in cartoons where the character has to decide between a good choice and a bad choice. They have an angel on one shoulder and a devil on the other and both of them are saying different things. This felt the same except that, oddly, the angel and the devil kept switching sides.

First, the angel said, "Remember your principle? You're not talking to him because you promised you wouldn't. Do you really want to go back on your word for a party? You've got no integrity."

The devil answered: "Come on, it's a party. Just say whatever you have to say and you'll get to go. Who cares about principles and promises and yada yada yada. Just go talk to your dad already."

You would think at this point the angel would have argued back to the devil, but to my surprise he (or she — who knew?) actually agreed. "Well, Coco, you know it's the right thing to go to talk to your dad. You can't be angry with him forever. Are you going to still not be talking to him when you're eighteen? Are you enjoying this? Really? You must be missing him, even just a little bit."

Just to make it all more confusing, the devil then disagreed. "No, don't talk to him. You're mad. Stay mad.

Punish him for wrecking your life."

"Shut up already!" I said—out loud. I had a quick look around to make sure no one was looking. "I can't even think."

But then I decided. And it was a decision that was purely based on what was practical. I *would* ask Dad. I did want to go the party, plus it was kind of annoying not being able to talk to him here and there, especially when Mum was out and I needed to know where the bread was or if the phone was charged or something important like that. As for the principle, well, I'd kept my word for like, nearly nine months, which is pretty impressive when you think about it. The only thing I didn't want to deal with was the second last reason. "You can't live angry with him forever."

*Maybe that's true*, I thought, *but I'm not ready to forgive him just yet. I'm just asking to go to a party. How hard can it be?*

It was harder than I thought.

I walked up to the house site. Dad was kneeling on the concrete slab messing around with some mortar. I stood about two metres from him.

"Dad," I said. "Hey, Dad."

He looked up and around and when he saw it was me his face looked confused. His eyes shifted from side to side, like he was checking that he'd heard right.

"Dad," I said. "Can I talk to you?" Now I suddenly felt nervous. I kicked the toe of my gumboot on the ground and chewed my lips.

"Hang on," he said. He put down his trowel and wiped his fingers on his pants. Then he stood up, all the way up. I had forgotten how tall he was.

He stood there for a minute, just quiet. The silence between us seemed to be swaying, vibrating almost, with its own aliveness. He kept waiting. He didn't say anything. He just stood and looked at me, but his face wasn't angry. It wasn't even impatient, or expectant or needy or anything else you might have thought. He just kind of looked at me like he was seeing me again for the first time. Or maybe it was that he had been seeing me for a long time, but I'd never noticed it. Maybe it was me seeing him seeing me for the first time. Or something. Whatever it was, it was warm. And rich. And full.

And all of a sudden I could see that inside me was an enormous dark, raging pit and I knew that was the place where I was angry but I also knew that whatever it was I was getting from Dad at that exact minute could help to fill it up and I nearly wanted to cry.

But I held it together.

"Um, Dad. I wanted to ask you a question," I said. I could see the corners of his mouth starting to curl up but he was trying to control it, just like me.

"Sure," he said. He waited some more.

"It's about a party in Sydney my friends are having. Mum said if I asked you, I could go."

He was still looking at me, still warm. Now my mouth was starting to curl into a smile and we were both just kind of half smiling at each other like we both got the hidden joke in all of this but we were going to keep it as our secret.

"No problem," he said, finally. "Do you want me to take you up and bring you back again?"

"If you like," I said. And then I thought for another minute and spoke again. "Yeah. That would be nice."

And I turned and ran back to the shed but as I did, I looked back and I could see that his face was one big grin and then mine was too and it was weird but it felt like my body was actually lighter and I could run quicker because of it and the big black pit of rage inside was slightly smaller and less scary because really, when it comes down to it, if you and your dad are friends again, there's not that much that can frighten you.

# CHAPTER 23

The day of the party was beautiful. The sun was sparkling in the sky and the rain we'd had a week ago had made everything green.

"Perfect day for Pony Camp," said Charlie, pulling on her jodhpurs. She was still mad with me. I could tell. For one thing she kept avoiding looking at my face. I was determined to show her I didn't care, that she could be as immature as she liked. I wasn't going to be bothered.

"Perfect day for a party too," I said, a little bit snarky. "Even better with harbour views."

"Huh," she said. "We've got river views."

"I hope you have fun," I said, and I genuinely meant it, no matter how mean she was being. I felt kind of righteous inside, like a misunderstood saint. The day was beautiful, I was going to Sydney, and even though Charlie was mad with me for no real reason that I could see, I was friends with Dad again. It was easy to be nice. Maybe this was my gift of love Ness talked about. "I really do. I'm kind of sad to miss it. Is anyone going to ride Cupcake?"

"Pfft," said Charlie. "Like you care. Someone will ride

her. It just won't be you."

"I hope they're okay to her," I said, still righteous and forbearing.

Charlie made an exasperated noise. "She'll be fine," she said. "She's been great for ages. You're not going to be there so you don't have to pretend to be concerned about it."

I nearly lost my cool with her then and there and was just about to tell her that I had every right to be concerned, that if anyone was going to be concerned about it, it should be me because who else had spent all those hours in the round yard with her and that I hoped she didn't ride Cupcake because, honestly, I didn't think the two of them were compatible at all but I was interrupted before I could begin.

"Coco," yelled Dad from across the shed. "Are you getting ready to go?"

"Better get my stuff," I said to Charlie in a huff. "We're heading off in ten minutes." I grabbed my clothes and put everything into an overnight bag. I was going to get changed before the party — there was no point in sitting in the car for two hours getting sweaty and crushed.

It had taken me two whole days to decide what to wear. I had pulled my suitcase up onto my bed, taken everything out and then laid out as many different combinations of shirts, pants, shorts, skirts and dresses as I could think of. Mum laughed when I told her I calculated that with six pairs of pants, twelve tops, seven dresses, nine skirts, three pairs of shoes and eight basic accessories I had about 108,000 possible outfits to choose from. (I'm sure that's not realistically true though. I mean, that would mean one of the outfits would simply be a pair of shoes or earrings and nothing else, which would be extremely high on the 'ick' factor.)

Anyway, I'd tried on look after look and taken selfies on my iPod with my arm right up high so I could just about see the whole outfit in the one shot. Charlie refused to help me. She was reading a horse book Tessa had lent her.

Finally I settled on some pointy toed flats and a dress I'd bought just before we left Sydney. I'd only worn it once, which was definitely not enough because it was gorgeous — a pink toned cotton dress with roses on it and a bow at the back. Perfect for a peasant style hairdo. Or a low messy bun. Or, actually, a whole bunch of other hairstyles. It occurred to me that perhaps I should have upped the calculations to literally a million different looks, based on adding in the hair possibilities.

"That looks great," Dad had said, as I swirled in front of him. "Perfect. I'm sure you'll have fun. There are parents going to be there, right?"

"Yes, Dad, don't worry! It's all good," I said.

"Is Alexandra going to be there?" he said.

"Alexandra?" I said. "Who's Alexandra?"

"You know, that friend of yours who I met once or twice."

"You mean Samantha," I said. I gave him the half roll but it was friendly. "And it wasn't just once or twice. It was like twenty times. She was always over at our place."

"Oh," he said. "Really?" His voice trailed off. "I guess I was thinking about something else every time... but I'm sure I'll recognise her when we see her."

I don't know how many times my dad has been wrong in the last ten months, but he was wrong again this time too. He had no idea who the girl was who was waving and — there is only one accurate word for it — simpering at us, when we finally pulled up outside Saffron's house in Vaucluse late in the afternoon.

The really surprising thing was that I didn't recognise her myself. Samantha had been an average-height blonde with straight, long hair when I had left. This girl was tall, willowy and a brunette. And she was wearing clothes that looked they'd walked straight out of Teen Vogue and had been all grunged down to prove a point. But then she smiled and straight away I knew it was her.

"Helloooo Pumpkin," I said, jumping out of the car and heading towards her for a hug. She smiled and then wavered. I was confused. Did we not hug now? She answered my question by giving me an air kiss on one cheek, and then suddenly moving to the other side for a second. She patted my shoulder briefly and then broke away.

"Coco! Look at you!" she said. And she was. Looking me up and down, that is. Top to bottom. And without a happy expression on her face. "You look so... sweet. That's great. It's nice to see you back." She wrestled a smile to her face. "Come on in. I've been sitting out here waiting for you."

I waved at Dad. "Later. I'll call you, okay?" He waved and drove off and Samantha and I turned towards Saffron's Very. Very. Very. Impressive. House. The walls were white, the gates were silver and the garden looked like it had just been vacuumed.

"Does she seriously live here?" I giggled. "This is incredible."

"Yeah, it's pretty good," said Sam, shrugging. "We always come here on weekends."

She pressed the intercom button, waited for a second and said, "It's me, Sammi. She's here."

The gates swung open automatically and we went through. I took a deep breath in and clutched Samantha's arm. "I'm so excited. This is how life is supposed to be. Parties, friends and in the city! I feel like I'm back."

Samantha smiled. But it was a dim smile. And it was right then, exactly at that point, that I began to get nervous.

If there were two words to describe Saffron's house, apart from 'impressive', they would be 'big' and 'white'. Everything was white — carpet, walls, ceilings, furniture, blinds, cushions, vases, flowers — everything. The kitchen was white and shiny. The main lounge room was white and furry. The only things that weren't white were a huge black chandelier and the view. This house had serious harbour views.

I followed Sam out onto the balcony. Just like the front yard, it looked like it had been dusted and polished by a team of gardeners, all with obsessive-compulsive disorder. All I wanted to do was give big, round-eyed gasps about the house, but Sam just kept walking as though it was nothing special, down the steps and out to where a group of people was standing beside the most sparkly, diamond-white swimming pool I had ever seen in my life.

I couldn't help myself. "Wow." It popped out of

my mouth involuntarily. And then it happened again. "Wow." Because just at that moment, the group of boys and girls parted and I saw Saffron.

She looked as shimmery as the pool behind her. Her blonde hair was glowing in the sun and her clothes looked like they'd been flown in from fashion heaven exclusively for her. Immediately I could see that Sam's look was a sad copy. Beside Saffron was Tiger Lily, now with flaming red hair and an outfit that was all Rock Chick meets Glam Princess but with hipster overtones.

"Hey you guys!" I said warmly. I felt almost teary with happiness. "It's so great to see you."

Saffron stepped forward. "Coco," she said with outstretched hands. She came towards me and air kissed both my cheeks. "You're here." She stepped back and did the looking up and down thing like Sam had already done. There was a look in her eyes I couldn't quite read.

Tiger followed Saffron out of the group. Her eyes also gave me the once over. "I see you've decided to go retro." She pursed up her lips. "That's... cute."

My smile shrivelled up. I had to fight the look of horror that wanted to replace it. My dress was wrong! And I hadn't seen it until this second. How could I have been so stupid? Of course styles were going to change. I mean, I had been away for practically a whole year. Even if wearing a dress had been the right thing (which it clearly wasn't), this was completely the wrong dress. The roses were the wrong size and the colours were glaring. When I looked at my feet I saw that my shoes were wrong too. Everyone else was in roman sandals or teetering on platform heels. Pointy-toed flats were definitely not being worn this season. I nervously clenched my fists and stretched my fingers and that was when I saw a smirk come over Tiger Lily's face. I looked down at my hands to see my worst nightmare. There was dirt under my nails.

I might have turned then and there and run away, except for Isabella. She shook off the boys around her and came out to hug me, wobbling on heels that were higher than a small stack of books.

"Coco!" she said. "You're here! When Saffron told me that you'd be coming, I was so excited! It's been so long since we saw you. How was the school! Did you ever get put in solitary? Was it really strict? Are you back now? Will you be coming back to school next year? You've got such a great tan, I can't believe it!"

I smiled her a weak 'thank you' with my eyes and accepted the hug gratefully. "Um, it was good, it was okay," I said. "I'm not quite back yet, but nearly."

She slapped her forehead. "Oh, I should have asked. Do you want a drink? Some food? I brought these amazing lime and chilli chips. Have you had them before? My mum got them from the Italian grocer. They're like, practically calorie-free. Soooo good."

"Let's all go and get a drink," said Saffron, and Isabella shrank back a little. Saffron still had a very odd look on her face. "I need something to refresh me."

She led the way up the stairs, through the balcony area, into the white fluffy lounge room and all the way through to the enormous kitchen. Even in our old house in Randwick, which had a pretty big kitchen, I had never seen so much shining, clear counter space in my life.

The kitchen was empty, apart from food laid out on one section of the bench. Something seemed to be missing. The group was talking and laughing behind me and I turned to Isabella and asked, quietly so no one else would hear, "Is Saffron's mum here? Who's doing the food?" Isabella looked at me puzzled. "She's never here when we come over. Saff doesn't let her stay." She pulled my arm. "Look, here are the chips. They're low-fat so you can have a few at least."

I nibbled on a chip. "Yummy," I said. They were good. But the lime and chilli flavour didn't take away the uncomfortable feeling in my stomach.

"So, how was your school?" said Saffron, suddenly whirling around to face me. "It must have been incredible!" She put a lot of emphasis on the word incredible. "Did you learn everything about riding? Make heaps of friends?" She smiled at me and for some reason it reminded me of the smiles of the air hostesses on the plane when we had a family holiday to Fiji a few years back. All mouth, no eyes.

"Oh, it was okay," I said. I was nervous, trying to bluff. "I did some riding. But there was no one there like you guys. I'll be coming back to school next year, probably as a boarder." I grabbed a piece of sushi. "Um, are there drinks?"

Tiger Lily gestured to the fridge. "Help yourself," she said, shrugging. I opened it but all I could see was beer. I looked around, confused and then noticed that all the boys were holding cans in their hands. The girls were drinking from cups, but it didn't look like it was lemonade. *I'm not drinking that*, I thought. *I didn't think this would be that kind of party. Now what am I going to do?*

I could feel prickles of sweat breaking out across my shoulders. I could hardly close the fridge and not have a drink now, having asked for one. Thankfully, at the last second, down on the very bottom shelf, I saw three bottles of mineral water and a can of creaming soda.

I hate mineral water, but I despise creaming soda more so I grabbed the least bad choice and shut the fridge.

"Just mineral water?" said Tiger Lily, laughing, but not in a good way. "This is a party, right?" She walked up to the fridge, grabbed a beer and opened it in one swift seamless motion. Even Dad couldn't have done it like that. Then she swigged it and held it out to me. "Want some?"

I shook my head. "I'm good for now, thanks," and gave a nervous laugh. "Heh heh." I turned away so she wouldn't see the red in my face. It wasn't so much from embarrassment as from confusion. I'd been expecting more fun and less, I don't know... attitude? Somehow it wasn't feeling like a party. Maybe my friends just hadn't warmed up to me yet.

And anyway, surely it couldn't get any worse?

Ha.

It was at that point that the doorbell rang.

"Oooh, they're here," gushed Saffron, plunging for the door. Before she turned the handle she looked around at the group and I saw a knowing glance and secret smile pass between her and Tiger. "Hey everyone, here's Darcy!"

When I heard his name all my arm hair stood up at attention and I suddenly couldn't breathe. Of course.

Darcy. How could I have forgotten? This was the moment I'd been waiting for, for nearly a whole year. My imagination went into overdrive. Maybe this would be the moment I fell in love across a crowded room, just like in the movies. If it was going to happen, I was ready. Although I kind of wished I wasn't wearing the so-very-obviously-out-of-fashion pink dress. Even jeans would have been better. But it was too late to worry about that because the door opened.

And in walked Darcy.

Or maybe it wasn't.

I squinted my eyes and furrowed my eyebrows. Was that him? He was a dark-haired boy and he swaggered across the room, letting Saffron give him a giggling kiss on the cheek and hugging Samantha. But it couldn't have been Darcy, because for some reason I recognised him. I'd seen him before, and not just in a photograph. My mind had to tick a few beats before it worked out where. And when the answer finally came I had to seriously control my mouth from giving a very loud yelp.

Darcy was Dee. Arrogant, good looking Dee from the horse ride. The one I'd drooled over. The one who'd creeped out Tessa and made her cry. The one who James had warned off, and told me to stay away from.

I felt wobbly. Like I'd had my chair pulled out from under me. This wasn't supposed to be happening. Dee was Darcy? Darcy was Dee? Where was my dreamboat from the photograph I'd seen? Where was my hero from my Jane Austen novel?

But I had more important things to think about than Jane Austen right now. Darcy/Dee was heading to my end of the room and I didn't want to talk to him. Not until I'd figured out a plan of attack. I tried to hide behind Samantha and an armchair (white of course) and look like I was casually not there. But it didn't work.

Darcy saw me.

And he came right over to me.

And then it was like one of those ads on TV where they slow the action right down and the audience slowly watches the orange juice fall or the car crash into the truck or whatever disaster it is that they are showing as if there's nothing else happening in the entire world right that millisecond.

Because everyone was watching Darcy. And everyone was watching Darcy watch me. I could see a look of recognition come over his face.

"Hey," he said. But it wasn't a nice 'hey'. It had lots and lots of meaning in it. He opened his mouth slightly and kind of caught his lip between his teeth and then let it go. Slowly.

Then he smiled. But it wasn't a nice smile. (This was beginning to be kind of a theme.) It was a smile with lots and lots of intention in it.

"Hey. Coco, right?" he said.

I nodded. Slowly. Miserably. Embarrassedly. (And yes, I know that's not a proper word but it really should be.)

"You're into horses, right?" he said. He grinned wider. It wasn't a nice grin. "I bet you're good at riding. Just like your friend. Tessa, isn't it?"

I didn't know what to do. My heart was racing. This was not good. This was all wrong. I kind of squeaked a reply but I don't even know what it was — maybe a 'yes/no' combination which may have turned out to be a 'yo'. But it didn't seem to move him. He just stood there, still looking at me.

Before now, I had never realised that being looked at could be creepy and gross and icky. I suddenly needed to go to the bathroom and wash something. Anything.

"Um, gotta go," I said. I quickly squeezed out from behind the armchair and passed Samantha, who was now hanging off Darcy's arm, and ran down the hall looking into door after door for the bathroom.

It was the seventh door on the left, if you can believe that. And it was so perfectly gleaming white I could just about see myself in the tiles. But I wasn't in the mood to check out my appearance. My head was spinning. I had to breathe. A lot. I felt ill, grossed out and mortified. My great come-back had turned into a great big fail. I was wearing the wrong dress, I was drinking the wrong thing and I was reacting the wrong way to the most popular boy in the room.

*Pull yourself together,* I scolded myself. *This is all part of being popular. You're just obviously out of practice and they all just need some time to warm up — I mean, they haven't seen you for like, nearly a year. And you can avoid Darcy for now, at least until you figure all this out.*

I took a few deep breaths and opened my eyes really big a few times in the mirror, just in case any extra tears had collected there, ready to spill out at some inopportune time. I shook myself a little, straightened my dress and sorted myself out.

"Come on Coco. This is a party. You can be fun, witty

and beautiful. You belong here," I said, but quietly, just in case anyone was walking too close to the door outside. "Make it work."

I walked back down the hallway towards the lounge room. The door was open but the sound seemed different. When I'd fled, five minutes before, people were laughing and talking and clinking their drinks. Now it was quiet.

Completely quiet.

Which was weird.

*It's nothing. They've all probably just gone outside, onto the balcony or something,* I thought. *I'll go and look out there.*

I took a few steps forward and then I heard a 'click' behind me.

Which was also weird.

I turned around to see Darcy standing with his back against the door. He was grinning. Kind of. It was less of a grin and more of a leer.

"Cute dress, Coco."

"Where did everyone go?" I asked.

"Does it matter?" he said.

"Um, yeah," I said, anxious. "I just want to find the others."

"They wanted us to get to know each other," he said, shrugging. "They've headed outside."

"I want to go too," I said. My voice went high. "The view is good."

"They said you were part of their group," he said. He took a step closer to me. "Just my type."

"I don't know anything about that," I said, looking around nervously. "Come on, let's go outside."

"Stay here with me," he said. "Let's sit down."

He grabbed my arm and headed towards the couch and in a flash all I could see was Tessa in the bush, crying, and Darcy's thunderous face and James' tight lips and I knew that James had been right. I should stay away from this guy.

"No!" I shouted and kicked him in the shins. Pointy-toed flats might not have been in fashion, but they obviously had some bite because he was so surprised that he let go of me, swearing and holding his leg. I nearly turned and said sorry but then I realised that would be stupid so I ran to the door leading to the outdoor area. I gave it a few hard pulls and then realised it was locked so I fiddled with the clips and bolts and, just as Darcy was getting up again (with the same angry face I'd seen before), I flipped it open and ran outside.

*I've got to find Sam,* I thought desperately. *She'll know what to do. Things can't get any worse than this.*

Which is, as I've said, time and time again, an incredibly stupid thing to say. Because every time I do, things seem to get worse.

A lot worse.

When I ran out onto the patio, my friends turned from their conversations and stared at me. I looked back at them. And then I realised. They did not have welcoming looks on their faces.

Tiger Lily, especially.

"So. Did you like Darcy?" she said, stepping forward. "Have fun in there?" A trickle of laughter went around.

"What?" I said.

"You heard me. Did you have fun with Darcy? Because

you were really into him a year ago. So we thought we'd set it up for you."

I blinked a couple of times. And then I looked at Samantha for help. "Do you know...?" But my voice trailed off because she looked away from me. Deliberately away. And then I saw that everyone else was watching us. Like something big was about to happen.

I heard Isabella's voice, half-hearted and quiet from behind me. "Don't do this to her," she said. "Come on."

"Why not?" said Tiger Lily, still clear and loud. "She broke the rules."

"What?" I said. I was confused and terrified and trapped. "No... no I didn't."

"Yes. Yes you did," said Tiger. She was mocking me. Saffron came to stand beside her. Her voice was much more reasonable.

"We let you into our group," she said. She sounded soothing. Almost nice. "We made you popular and beautiful."

"...yeah, even though you're not that pretty," said Tiger Lily.

"And then," Saffron shrugged, "you broke our rules. And you lied to us."

I tried again. "I didn't..." but I knew I did.

"Really? You didn't?" said Tiger Lily. "What's this?"

She pulled out her phone and held it up to my face. There was a photo on it. Of me. In gumboots. Covered in mud. In Kangaroo Valley.

"That was you who took that picture that day? I didn't even see you." I said to Tiger Lily.

"Your sister did though," she said. "What did you

think? That no one would ever find out you were lying to us? You're a nobody. I mean, really, Kangaroo Valley?"

I was still looking for help. Even in unlikely places. "Sam? You told them?" I half whispered it.

"Sammi had nothing to do with it," said Saffron. "She's out of the picture." Now her voice was cutting and clear.

But Samantha stepped up. Her voice was extra-sweet. It kind of reminded me of when she told me that purple didn't suit me.

"It wasn't my idea to lie in the first place," she said. "I just wanted to do the best by Saff and Ti and the others." She looked around at them. "If you can't be a true friend and do what you've agreed to do, then you kind of, you know, get what you deserve." She shrugged. "I'm sorry, but you've brought it on yourself."

I felt like the world was spinning. These were my friends. Dropping me. In public. I was still trying to get my head around it and my body wouldn't cooperate. I chewed my lips, stood on one leg and then the other, shrugged my shoulders, adjusted my posture and looked around me from side to side. My eye caught a movement. It was Darcy coming out onto the balcony. He winked. I shuddered and nearly retched.

"She didn't want to play with me," he called out to Saffron as he walked down to the pool, making a face like a surprised child.

Saffron made a face at me. It was elegant and beautiful, but it was still a face. "Oh dear," she said. "You won't drink, won't play and you look terrible. I'm afraid you're not good enough for us." She shrugged. "Although really, you never were. You were always our sympathy makeover person. We were a bit bored and we wanted a project so we picked you. But now we're dropping you." She tilted her head. "Sorry."

She turned away and went to giggle in Darcy's ear. But my lecture wasn't over yet. Tiger Lily stepped forward.

"By the way, if you ever come back to St Agnes, we'll be making sure you're a lot worse off than that fat loser Shannon. She changed schools, she was so miserable. But we know people where she goes now, so I made sure they heard about her. It's not going to end." She shrugged. "I guess the point is, you can't come back here. Looks like you'll be living in Wombat Hole forever."

"Kangaroo Valley!" I said. It was through tears. I couldn't help it. They were running down my face. *I can't believe this is happening,* I thought. *Surely I can still change it.*

"But you were so keen for me to come tonight," I said, pleading.

"We lied," said Saffron, smiling, still hanging on to Darcy's arm.

"Fair's fair, right?" said Tiger Lily. "I mean, you lied to us first."

"Oh, and by the way?" said Darcy. "You probably really need to do something about your teeth. I wouldn't actually want to kiss you. Kind of gross." He screwed up his face and looked down at Saffron. "You, on the other hand..."

Everything had hurt, but the crack about my teeth hit me low in the stomach. I couldn't breathe, I could hardly see through tears and I felt like doubling over to protect myself. *How can I get out of here?* I thought. *I need to get out of here.* But it wasn't over yet. As I turned around, looking for an exit I felt hands on my back, pushing me. The pressure was firm, and then stronger. I couldn't resist it and my whole body had to move. And then I was toppling and tossing and falling.

Right into the pool.

I swallowed water and came up, coughing, spluttering and panting for breath. It's nearly impossible to breathe when you're crying at the same time. I rubbed the water out of my eyes and looked up and that was when I heard it. Everyone was laughing. At me.

There was no way to salvage any of this. It was over. I climbed out of the pool and ran, tripping over, dripping water through the house, heading out the front door. In the front yard I scrabbled in my bag for the phone Mum had given me. At least that hadn't gotten wet. Inside I could hear them laughing and high fiving and turning up the music.

I dialled Dad's number and paced while the connection was made. Everything always is so slow when you're desperate to escape. I manically tried to wipe the drips from my hands off the phone, but I had nothing dry to soak them up with and I was about to start crying all over again when Dad's voice came on the line.

"Dad?" I sniffled, gulping like a fish. "Dad? Can you come get me? Please." I burst into tears.

"Coco? Is that you? Are you okay?" he said. His voice was worried.

"I'm okay. Just come get me right now. Right now!" I said, snuffling and sobbing and gasping for breath.

It takes thirteen minutes to get to Vaucluse from Bondi, and those thirteen minutes were definitely the longest of my life. I didn't want to wait on the street because I was worried about creepy people who might hurt me, but I'd just come from a party full of creepy people who had already hurt me so I couldn't wait inside. In the end I sat next to the gate, trying to hide behind a bush, and cried and cried.

At one point Isabella came out with a towel and half heartedly handed it to me. "Here you go. Just to get the water off." She stood awkwardly, waiting for me to finish.

"Thanks," I said. I could hardly look at her.

"I'm sorry," she said. "I actually always liked you, but..." She shrugged and gestured with her head but I ignored her and there was nothing else to say so she went back in to the party.

When Dad finally arrived I fell into his arms. His hug was strong and a huge relief.

"What's going on?" he said. "Are you okay?" He made a move to go inside. "Where's everyone?"

"Let's just go, just go." I said, pulling him out onto the street and away from the front door. Away from the ugliest house in the world. "Where's the car? We have to go."

"You're wet." He looked down. "You're soaking. Did someone hurt you?" I could hear the concern in his voice.

"No, not hurt." I said. I was desperate to leave. "I'm okay. I just fell in the pool by mistake. It was just..." I shook my head. "I don't know... embarrassing." I saw a question in his face and I shook my head. "No. I can't talk about it. Please. Let's just go."

He hesitated again. "Are you sure? Shouldn't I speak to the parents? Do they know what's going on?"

"No. I just want to get out of here," I said. "Please Dad. Talk to someone later if you have to. Just not now."

"Okay," he said. He looked towards the door one last time and then his face made a decision. "Okay, let's go."

We got into the car and sat there for a minute. My dress made the seat wet. It was going to be a long uncomfortable drive. I put on my seatbelt.

"Do you want to talk about it?" he asked.

"No," I said. "I just want to go back to the farm."

# CHAPTER 24

Dad was nice. It was the first time I had thought that in a whole year but it was true. At first he wanted to take me back to Bondi but I insisted that we didn't stay with his friends that night. In fact, I wouldn't even get out of the car.

"No, I just want to go. Please Dad, just take me back to the farm," I said. He must have listened to the urgency in my voice because he didn't even try to make me stay. Instead he just went in, made an apology to his friends, picked up our stuff and came back to the car.

"We won't be home until late," he said. "Can you do that?"

I nodded mutely. I could do anything as long as it meant I was out of range of Saffron and Tiger and Samantha and Darcy. I could even listen to soft pop radio and tolerate Dad singing along to the 'best of the 80s and 90s'. We drove and drove and I put up with the fact that my tongue was dry and my mouth was raw and I felt like someone had punched me in the lungs. It was hard to get a full breath. Plus my legs were wet and my dress was sticking, clammy, to me.

"You alright, Coco?" said Dad.

"I'm okay," I said. But I wasn't. I was a loser, I was ugly, I had no future and my dreams of being somebody, being special and being significant had been bashed on a rock and left to die in the cold.

"It's not long now." Dad spoke again. "Another forty minutes or so. We'll be home soon."

I let out a silent, bitter laugh. Home? My home was back in Sydney, or so I'd thought. For a whole year I'd held on to the idea that home was somewhere else, that the farm was temporary. I didn't belong there. I'd put up with it for a while but ultimately, I thought, I was headed back to the place I belonged.

It's just that now I didn't belong there. Or anywhere. I'd been dumped by my group, I'd been betrayed by my best friend and I'd been let down in my hopes for Darcy. It wasn't as if I had any other friends in Sydney either. Ever since Year Seven, Samantha and I had completely pinned our hopes on Saffron's clique and ignored everyone else at school.

In Budgong, all that was waiting for me were my extra-special-at-everything-she-does twin sister, my annoying brother who didn't even like me, and Tessa and James who were nice enough, but ordinary. But I'd dumped them, and in a terrible way. And they were all mad at me. It would be too much to ask them to have me back.

Outside the car window the moon was big, gold and hanging low in the sky. All I noticed was how little I was in comparison. I leaned my head against the car window. I had no energy to sit up and I had no energy to keep my anger and my betrayal hidden inside me. I sat there with my head cool on the window glass and tears falling out of my eyes onto my damp dress, running down my legs to the floor.

If Dad noticed, he didn't say anything.

"Do you mind if we stop by the stables, sweetheart?" he said when we were nearly there. "Mum doesn't have her phone with her and I need to tell her that we're back. Is that okay?"

I nodded, silent. When we pulled up I stayed in the car. "I don't really want to come in," I said. "I'm too tired."

"That's okay," he said. "I'll be about five minutes." He shut the door behind him and I sat, alone in the car, with the radio off. The silence reached up and pawed at my face until I slapped it away and opened my window. But that was the wrong decision. From the old building behind the stables I could hear giggles, warm voices and happy music.

My stomach ached, but it was with regret. I wanted to see what I had missed at Pony Camp, what I had thrown away as worthless. With my phone in my hand, I got out of the car and walked over to the window.

It was another wrong decision.

Inside were twenty five teenagers, sitting around chatting, laughing and playing cards. The kerosene lanterns shone a warm glow on their faces. I could see Tessa and Charlie and Josh sitting together, with James a little apart. His eyes were on Charlie and he had a half-smile on his face. It looked like a party—but a real one. A good one.

I took a breath in and gulped back a sob. My neck hurt and my head felt like it had a million tiny pins pricking into it. *It's not fair*, I began to say to myself. *Nobody cares about me. Why do I have to suffer so much?*

At that exact moment I felt the familiar purr of the phone in my hand. Immediately I was on alert. Who could be calling? And at this time? The only person I'd given the number to was Samantha, before the party, just in case she needed to get in touch. I doubted any of Mum's friends would be ringing at midnight. I took a sudden breath. If it was Sam, surely it could only be good. Maybe she was ringing to apologise or to say that there had been some terrible misunderstanding.

I hardly dared to hope. I glanced down at the phone in my hand. It was a text. And it was from Samantha.

And she was saying sorry.

*Really?*

I read it. And then I read it again.

**Hey Coco. Sorry about before. Are you dry yet? BTW I had to drop you. Dead if I didn't. You understand, right?**

My last hope had gone. It had been blown out like a little kid blows out her birthday candles, with a heavy dose of accidental spit. Sorry? Had to? Understand? Fire started in my heels and flowed in my veins all the way to my head. My rage was building. Was Sam for real? I had thought we were friends. Best friends. Real friends.

I could see her face when they had dropped me. It was smarmy, smiling, triumphant, like it was the easiest thing in the world to do. A sudden thought overtook my brain. I grabbed the phone and pressed reply.

Was it you who pushed me in the pool?

Her reply took less than four seconds. I was counting.

Oops. It just kinda happened.

And then in another second.
Darcy's here. He still thinks u r cute.

It was then, right there, at that point that I could
have screamed. But I didn't. Because I was so angry I
was beyond screaming. I was shaking. I was trembling.
I was shivering, even though it was warm. My hands
lost their control and I dropped my phone into the dark
of the ground, but it didn't matter. I was never going to
text Samantha again. Or anyone else. Because I had no
friends. And no hope of ever having any.

No. That wasn't true. I had one friend. The best kind.
The kind that was never going to betray me. And she
was just here in the stables.

I ran across the grass in the dark and moved the
heavy latch to open the stable door. The lock creaked but
I hardly noticed. My thoughts were flying around and I
was muttering and talking to myself, almost sobbing. *I've
just got to get Cupcake, I'm going to get Cupcake*, I said, over
and over. Something inside me was insisting that if I just
went for a ride, everything would be okay. The anger
and rage and energy that were fizzing like a shaken soda
can would fly away into the air if I galloped with strong,

warm Cupcake who could hold me up and make me okay again.

Cupcake was at the back of the stable, eating some hay. When I found her I buried my head in her neck. She nickered in recognition and nudged me with her head. I grabbed her bridle and it felt solid and secure in my hand. "You can see in the dark, right girl?" I said, quietly. "Want to go out with me?" I grabbed a helmet from the hook, latched it on and led Cupcake out of the door. The warm breeze was starting to turn chilly but I didn't care. I could hardly think straight. I just knew I needed to get away.

Inside everyone was still laughing and joking and sitting by lamplight. I looked over at the windows shining their golden, warm, happy light and bitterly hoisted myself up to Cupcake's bare back.

I leaned down to her ear to speak. "Come on," I said. "Let's go."

# CHAPTER 25

It would sound cute to say that Cupcake and I galloped into the sunset, but of course, it being the middle of the night, there was no sunset. And at first she was a little bit hesitant to gallop, but she got used to it quickly and I was urging her on, faster and faster. The anger in my body was being transferred to Cupcake's hooves. I just wanted to move, fly away, escape. I want to be by myself. It was pointless to be with others. No one would understand what had happened. No one had understood anything at all about my life up to this point. Not Dad, not Mum, not Josh. Not even Charlie.

*I hate you! I hate you all!* I yelled to the darkness. *Everything's gone! I can't do this anymore!*

We rode and rode and I was crying and my nose was streaming and I was gasping and screaming and raging. Every muscle in my body was aching to go harder, and Cupcake, like the wonderful girl she was, was taking all the anger for me, going faster and faster down the hill until it felt like we had taken off and were above the world, flying and floating right up to the moon.

My tears cleared and my body slumped, exhausted. I

leaned down and hugged Cupcake around the neck and brought her to a walk.

I looked up at the sky. The stars were out, like a cloud of fireflies buzzing. And the moon. I had never seen such a moon. It had been beautiful in the car, but to be outside in the air beneath it was like being part of a fireworks display. It was getting higher now and it had turned from pale gold to a deep silver. Occasionally it ducked behind a tree and I could see the branches and leaves as stark outlines against it.

I was still doing sniffy, gulping breaths but the rage had gone down. My whole body was spent. I felt like I had been tired for a long time.

Cupcake stopped to nibble the grass. I let her. It wouldn't hurt this once not to be strict. And maybe she was like me and needed to be given a break once in a while. While she munched, I had a little chat to the moon. It's funny to talk out loud to the sky but I figured someone or something would be listening.

"I just feel like nothing's fair," I said. "You probably saw it all happen. My friends dropped me, but really, it was only because I had to come and live out here. And that's not my fault. It's Dad's fault. If he hadn't wanted his stupid life change, we wouldn't be here and I would still be popular and everything would be okay." And I gave a short, sharp sigh.

The moon in all its shimmering glory looked back at me. And it didn't say anything.

I mean, I know that's what's meant to happen, right? The moon is not supposed to talk to you in the middle of the night when you're angry. It would be super-weird if it did, but I just wanted a little bit of understanding. Somehow I wanted a magic-moon-fairy-godmother type person to pop down from the sky and say, "Yes, Coco, this is all completely unfair and I will miraculously go back in time for you and fix it so that none of this ever happened. Oh and by the way, would you like a new dress? I see that yours is both wet and out of fashion. Ka-zing!"

With nothing but silence coming back to me, I got angry again. "Fine," I said. "If you won't help me, I'll fix it myself. Come on Cupcake, let's go."

I dug my heels into Cupcake. The entrance to the track up the cliff and over onto the dam was nearby. It was my favourite ride and I was going to take it. I pondered briefly about the fact that Dad might be looking for me and maybe I should go back, but I quickly got rid of the thought.

"Too bad," I said aloud. I was beginning to like this talking-to-the-sky thing. "It's his fault I'm in this state anyway. He can just wait. He's wrecked my life — what more does he want from me?"

I pushed Cupcake hard. She cantered up the mountain, panting and sweating, but now I didn't even care about her. I just wanted one thing — to get revenge on everyone. I wanted to make them look for me, to worry. I wanted them to pay some attention to me for once.

"Nobody ever thinks about me!" I yelled out loud. "Nobody cares! They just think they can ignore me and get away with it. Well, I'll show them."

We came off the top of the mountain onto a flat area that had a few different little streams and boggy patches.

I could tell that Cupcake wanted to slow down whenever we went near the water. She seemed nervous. But I just kept going and going, digging in my heels. When we got to one bigger place where she actually had to cross the stream, she shied at it and wouldn't go through. I got angry with her.

"Come on Cupcake. This is silly. Just do it." I yelled at her and slapped my reins across her shoulders. "Keep going! Go through the water."

And then I asked those fateful words, words which, I know now, will never cross my lips again. I said these words: "What could be worse than this?"

Yep.

Seriously.

You would think I would have learned.

But I hadn't.

The thing that could be worse than this was about to happen. Cupcake didn't want to step into the water. And then, a wombat, scared by all the noise of a crazy, yelling girl and a wild, galloping horse in the middle of the night, disturbing his quiet grass-eating, came running out of the bushes, straight into Cupcake's eye line. Cupcake saw the wombat.

Cupcake has never liked wombats.

When she saw it she shied, reared and bolted. As she jumped the stream, I fell backwards, and as I fell, my ankle twisted underneath me. All I could hear, as I landed on prickly, muddy scrub, was an enormous crack.

And that was when it all went black.

If they were making a movie of my life, this would be the point where the soft focus and the wobbly camerawork would come into play. I would flutter my eyelids a few times, say some nonsensical, but vaguely meaningful words and then open my eyes to focus right into the face of the person I love the most, whereupon I would smile and they would smile and wink back a few tears and whatever conflicts we had had up till that point would suddenly all be meaningless and completely over because just seeing each other again would be enough to solve every problem that had ever taken place.

It wasn't quite like that.

As I opened my eyes, all I could see was the moon laughing at me. All I could feel was shooting, sharp pain, moving upwards from my left foot but then quickly taking over my entire body. After about a minute the pain was so bad I threw up. All over my dress and on the ground. Then, because I couldn't hold up my head as it was both exhausting and painful, I put my head back on the ground and so of course my hair was covered with vomit.

I shut my eyes again. Perhaps it was all a bad dream. Perhaps when I next opened them I would magically be in a hospital, lying on clean white sheets, my hair washed and blow dried, with Wi-Fi available for my iPod and a TV playing comfortingly in the background.

I opened my eyes. It was still dark, scratchy and vomit-smelling. I winced. The pain from my foot was now becoming a serious throb, I was beginning to feel something decidedly uncomfortable in my ribs as well, and, even worse, I realised I was completely alone.

"Cupcake! Cupcake! Where are you?" I yelled. But my voice sounded pale and small, like one of those chipmunks on a YouTube clip. "Cupcake..." I pleaded. But there was no Cupcake. She was gone.

And I was left by myself in the dark and the cold.

# CHAPTER 26

I don't recommend sustaining a severe injury in the middle of the night in the back of the Australian bush. Basically, I don't really do pain that well. I tend to whimper and cry and plead into the darkness for it to go away. Plus, even though I was deliberately running away from everyone I knew, I don't really do 'alone' that well either.

Let me also say this. Those night noises that you hear in the forest? When you're on your own and you can't see anything and your brain feels like it's about to explode anyway, you really do begin to wonder if maybe there are things like vampires and werewolves and bloodsucking owls that could swoop down from the sky and take out your eyes, and the whole scenario kind of does weird things to your sanity.

Let's just say that by the time I was found, I was a quivering, blubbering, shivering, vomit-covered mess.

Obviously, it's not my preferred look.

Especially not when the person who finds you is a boy. And especially not when he's a boy who doesn't think that much of you anyway, especially not after you've insulted his sister and generally been a selfish idiot.

Yes, I was found by James. And Tessa. Embarrassment much?

"Coco! Coco?"

I had no idea how long it was before I heard their voices. I suppose it could have been only half an hour but it felt like about eight.

"Coco? Are you there?"

It always sounds like a cliché in books when people say that their hearts leap but when I heard Tessa's voice my heart did what I can only describe as a forward somersault handspring with a twist.

"Tessa? Is that you?" I squeaked out the words. It was amazing they could hear me but then I saw them riding down the hill and out of the bush.

"It's her! She's there!" Tessa yelled. She threw herself off her horse and knelt down beside me. "Over here, James. She's here. We found her."

"Stop talking, Tessa. Coco. Are you okay?" He got down from the horse and pulled out a flashlight and shone it in my face.

In normal circumstances I would have told him to get the light out of my face and to not worry. But these were not normal circumstances.

In these circumstances, filled with pain, covered in vomit and shaking with terror from the night, I did what any self-respecting girl would do.

I cried.

Big, shaking sobs with snot streaming out of my nose and slightly embarrassing shrieks of relief at being found.

"Oh, I love you so much. Thank you, thank you, thank

you. I can't believe you found me. I thought I was going to die. Cupcake just freaked out and reared and I just bounced off her back and then she ran away, and it really hurts, but I'm so glad you're here. Did I say I love you?"

The words just kept falling out of my mouth. Poor Tessa didn't know what to do except to hug me awkwardly. I held on to her hand like she was my saviour and didn't let her go. James stood back and waited.

"We've got to check that you're okay, Coco," he said, when I'd finally run out of breath. He knelt down beside me. "Do you think you can move?"

I rolled over towards him. Slowly. Painfully. "Maybe."

"I think if you can roll, there's probably no spinal injury," he said. "What about getting up?"

He put his arm around me to try to sit me up. I stiffened. I wasn't sure if it was going to work because the pain was so bad, but then I was sitting up, leaning against him.

"Ew. I'm so sorry. I think I smell of puke." I tried to pull away but he just laughed.

"It's not really any worse than cleaning up stables," he said. "I think I'll live. Can you stand up?"

"I'll try." I pushed down on the ground, clinging to his shirt but as soon as my ankle took any weight it felt like I was going to die. "Owwwwww!" I screeched. "Owah! Not possible."

"It's either broken or it's a really bad sprain," he said. I was still sobbing and whimpering on the ground. "Tess, if you ride back and tell them where we are, I'll stay here with Coco until they can get the car out here."

"What? You mean I can't come back with you? But

I need to go home!" I wailed at him. "I can sit on your horse with you." I suddenly felt desperate. I couldn't wait another hour.

"Well we can try," he said. "Want to stand up again? Tessa, you go on her other side."

*This time I'll manage*, I thought to myself. *I need to get home.* But my legs didn't want to cooperate and after two seconds I was back on the ground, crying again.

"Waaaah. It's hopeless. It's not fair," I sobbed. I felt like pounding my fists on the floor like a toddler, but everything hurt too much, plus I was now feeling bruises all down one side of my arm and on my bottom. And there was a sharp pain under my ribs where James had been supporting me. Crying was turning out to be too much work and then suddenly I realised that I had lost my audience. I rolled over stiffly to look at James, who had moved to sit away from me and was gazing at the moon. He turned to speak.

"Tessa's gone to get some help," he said mildly. "It will probably take an hour or more. I'll stay here so you can't run away again." He looked back at the moon. "Beautiful night tonight."

"You're not very sympathetic," I said. "I'm lying here in terrible pain and all you can say is that it's a beautiful night."

He sighed. "What did you want me to say?"

"Oh I don't know. Maybe something like, 'I'm so sorry you've broken your ankle. You poor thing. How can I help?'" My voice was sharp.

"Maybe you didn't realise this," he said, "but actually I am helping. I was having a perfectly good evening before having to come out into the cold and dark to look for someone. Especially a someone who's gone bareback riding on a difficult horse in a frilly summer dress in the middle of the night without telling anyone."

"You didn't have to," I said, sulking. "You could have stayed home."

"What kind of person do you think I am?" He sounded scornful. "I look out for my friends. I don't just leave them in the middle of the bush alone."

"Well I don't know. Whatever." I said. I struggled up onto one elbow and pulled myself up a bit. The pain was throbbing all the way down my leg. "Anyway, I've had a very difficult day. And I feel very upset."

"Is that why you ran away?" he said. He sounded unimpressed. "Because you felt upset?"

"You wouldn't say it like that if you knew what actually happened," I said. My voice was getting choked up. "My friends in Sydney dropped me."

"I thought you were going to a party," he said. "Why would your friends invite you to a party if they were dropping you?"

"I don't know." My chin wobbled. "They said they wanted revenge. And then I got pushed in the pool."

"Are you serious? Are they like, the mafia or something?" he asked. "Did you kill their parents or poison their dogs? Why on earth would they want to take revenge on you?"

"It's hard to explain," I said. "You wouldn't understand."

"Why not?" he said. He sounded genuinely curious.

"Because..." I said, but I couldn't go on. I wanted to

say, 'because you're ordinary, because you're not cool, because you're not popular, because you wear Cuban heels and ugly flannys,' but out in the open air, under a silver moon, sitting next to the boy who had left his own party to come to rescue me, my words suddenly sounded cheap, pathetic and nasty.

"I'm a person, just like you," he said. "And we've got at least an hour sitting here in the dark. You might as well try and make me understand."

So I told him all about it. I told him about Saffron and how much I admired her and her friends. I told him about the auditions and Sam and me trying so hard to get into the group. I told him about the fake school story we made up and the pretend rule about no emails and how desperately I'd been looking forward to going back to Sydney next year.

My words poured out of me, and I realised that I'd never actually told anyone any of this before. I'd kept it all in my own heart for a whole year, not sharing it with anyone. And through all of it, James sat and listened. He didn't talk, he didn't make fun of me, he didn't try and tell me I was wrong.

He just listened.

"And so I guess I was just really upset, and I saw you guys at the camp and I knew I had upset you and I thought I would never have any friends except Cupcake, and then even she left me when she got spooked..." My voice trailed off. I was nearly crying.

"But I still blame Dad."

"How is any of this your dad's fault?" James asked. He sounded genuinely puzzled.

"It's obvious, isn't it? If he had just let us all stay back in Sydney, none of this would have happened. I wouldn't have had to lie and I would have still been in the group and everything would be okay."

James looked at me. Even in the moonlight his blue eyes were clear and piercing. "No. I think you're wrong. Nothing would be okay if you were still in Sydney."

"What do you mean?"

"Don't you get it? If you were still in Sydney, you would still be with those girls and you would have become one of them."

"I don't understand."

"Coco, you're smart." He sounded frustrated. "I don't know why you don't get this. It's like you've got a blind spot. Those girls are mean. Look what they did to you at the party. And Samantha? Your 'best' friend? She pushed you in the pool. It doesn't matter what you might or might not have done to them, or if you 'broke' their rules. No one treats friends like that. Plus the guys they hang around with are really sleazy. I mean, like, completely gross. I know what kind of men they turn into, and believe me, it's not good." He shook his head in disbelief. "I think they've done you a complete favour by dropping you. If it was me, I wouldn't want to have anything to do with them."

"But..." My voice faltered. And then I suddenly knew that everything he was saying was right. My head was spinning. "But they're popular. And they're beautiful. And I want to be popular and beautiful."

"But you're popular already," said James. He shrugged his shoulders. "Anyway, why would you want to be popular if it means you treat people like they treated you?"

I thought for a second. "And like they treated Shannon..."

"Who's Shannon?" he asked.

"Another girl they dropped," I said quietly. Thoughtfully.

"Yeah, and they'll probably get rid of Samantha some time," he said, "or Isabella or whatever her name is — one of the other ones. Seriously, hanging around people like that doesn't do you any favours. You just need to have friends you like. People who like you."

When someone tells you a truth that you've never realised before, the words kind of echo in your head. Every word James said was like a bell, clanging in my empty brain. I could feel the reverberations right down to my feet, even the sore one.

But there was still a problem.

"But the whole point is that Charlie is just better than me at everything," I said. "Fashion and social stuff is the only thing I can do better than her. This is why I started hanging out with these people in the first place. Wherever we go, everyone admires Charlie more than me."

There was a silence. For a second James said nothing. The moon seemed bigger and the night sounds got quieter.

"I don't," he said.

My heart did another one of those tumble turn things. For a second I didn't breathe.

"What?" I said. But very quietly.

His answer was quiet too. "I don't admire Charlie

more than you."

I could hardly look at him. I was still focusing on the moon, but now instead of not being able to breathe, I had to control my breathing because it was getting faster and faster.

He kept talking. He also wasn't looking at me. Deliberately. "I don't know why you think you're no good at anything. You're amazing with Cupcake. You've got a real gift with horses. And you're funny. Apart from when you make major stuff ups in Truth or Dare, you've always got something clever to say."

He waited for a second.

"And you're really beautiful."

I just about choked. In a good way of course.

"Oh." I said. And shot him a sideways glance. He looked at me at the same time. It was like we were caught in the same silver stream of moonbeam for a beautiful, magical millisecond.

"Coco," he said. "I like you. You know, like, 'like like', not just like." And then he looked away, almost shy.

"Oh," I said again, and instinctively tried to move closer to him. "I really..." but as I spoke, I forgot I was injured and without thinking I shifted my weight onto my broken leg. The pain shot from my ankle to my hip, making me fall onto my hands, at which point my rib, which had been hurting a bit before suddenly went 'crack'.

Pain does funny things to you.

In my case, as I opened my mouth to tell James that I 'like liked' him as well, that I hadn't really noticed it until now even though I'd known it inside all along, that he was completely adorable as well as being right about me, and that I had a lot to learn and I was sorry for all the things I'd ever thought or said about him and especially his flannel shirts, which all of a sudden looked pretty good and not clichéd at all, out came a lot of something.

Out of my mouth came, not words, but puke. And it went straight into his lap.

# CHAPTER 27

Thankfully the next time I woke up it was in a hospital bed. My leg was in plaster, my finger was attached to a pinchy wire thing, a needle was sticking in my arm and there was stuff going *beep beep beep* around me. But the sheets were clean, there was a telly on in the corner and nothing hurt.

Best of all, Mum was there, looking worried and hovering over my face.

"Oh Mum!" I said. "I'm so sorry." And it was weird. You'd expect me to be crying or feeling bad but I was on top of the world. I gave her a Cheshire cat grin. "I shouldn't have run away or gone riding in the middle of the night. I didn't want you to be worried. And I'm sorry that I ended up here." My mouth couldn't stop smiling. "This is really weird. I should be feeling bad but I'm just really, really happy. Hee hee."

"That's the morphine," said Mum. I desperately wanted her to go in and out of focus like in the movies so I blinked a few times but she stayed herself.

"You've been a terrible worry," she said, smiling and shaking her head. "I nearly called the police last night and I was planning your funeral. I thought you'd been taken by a fox or eaten by a wombat or something. Or lost your brains and gone wandering and fallen into a dam and drowned." She patted my hair. "As it is, you've just broken your leg and cracked two ribs and you've got heaps of bruising all down your side. You've been in surgery and you're in recovery. But don't worry! You're smiling because of the drugs."

"No, I'm just smiling," I said and gave a little, involuntary giggle. Maybe it was the drugs. But I still felt like smiling. Because Mum was there, because I wasn't stuck out in the dark and the cold, because I was dry, because I was alive.

And of course, I was smiling because James thought I was beautiful.

I'd have to think about that some more, I decided. But not now. A bit later on. I was suddenly feeling very sleepy. And happy. And drowsy. And relaxed. Definitely later on. My face felt heavy and just as my eyelids hit my cheeks I noticed a definite fade out on mum's face.

"Excellent," I thought. "Finally. Some soft focus." And I promptly fell asleep.

Out of hospital and without the happy drugs, the rest of the recovery wasn't quite so fun. For a start, having a leg in plaster is heavy. And itchy! All I wanted to do was stick a knitting needle down the inside of it and give everything a good scratch but every time I tried it Josh told on me. "Mu-um, she's doing it again."

I'd stick out my tongue at him but I couldn't leave quickly (crutches are really slow) so I ended up having to stay in the same space and actually listen to him talking to Dad about the house and the ideas they had for the property.

"If we can possibly maximise the value of the rides and get more people coming, that would solve a lot of the financial issues," Dad said, frowning in thought. "But somehow we have to add value."

"You could always do rides at night," I said, laughing. "Even though it wasn't the greatest ride of my life, it was still really beautiful out there. You've obviously just got to watch out for wombats and water..."

Both Dad and Josh stopped, turned and looked at me. "That's a really good idea, Coco," said Josh. He looked slightly shocked. "You should actually think about that, Dad."

I smiled.

Because it was really hard to go down to the paddock on crutches, Mum offered to bring up Cupcake to see me every afternoon.

"It's okay," I said to her, nuzzling her nose, the first time she came. "It wasn't your fault. I was the crazy one for making you go out at night. I'm sorry for getting you into trouble, and I hope you weren't too scared when you ran home by yourself." She nickered reassuringly but took another carrot as if to say that I still owed her a few favours.

As I had to spend so much more time around the shed, unable to walk, I ended up helping Mum out in the kitchen most days.

"I finally got in touch with the dentist," she said one night as I was peeling carrots. "He said he doesn't usually bleach teeth before you're sixteen. The teeth have to be mature enough, apparently. If you don't mind, I'd rather you wait until then. I just don't want to do anything that's going to wreck them. You've got such a beautiful smile."

"That's okay," I said. "I guess I can wait. But it'll be the very day I turn sixteen, okay?" and I flashed her a toothy grin.

"The very day," she said. And she gave me a hug. "Oh, sorry, I forgot. I know those bruises hurt." But I hadn't pulled away in pain so I lifted up my shirt to check.

"Actually they're looking fine," I said. A little bit yellow still. But not the dark purple and deep red they'd been for two or three weeks after the Great Midnight Ride. I'd taken some pictures of them on my iPod and couldn't believe it when I looked back at them.

I'd also made up with Charlie. She was normally really quick to forgive me. In fact, I don't think we'd ever had a fight last for longer than a day but after the Truth or Dare fiasco with Tessa she'd been really upset.

At the hospital she'd had two main emotions. The first was relief that I was okay, but the second was determination to not let me think I was off the hook.

"Way to cause a fuss," she said, coming up to the side of my bed. I was still all hooked up to wires and tubes. "You really outdid yourself, even by your standards."

I looked at her. My smiley drugs had worn off and I had gotten back my ability to feel bad.

"Yeah, I guess." I said. "Charlie, I'm really..." but she cut me off.

"You know, I love you more than anyone in the world. Okay, maybe not more than Mum. But I definitely love you second. And when you love someone you have to tell them when they're in the wrong," she said. She looked worried. I didn't know what to say and plus my ribs were really aching so I just had to lie there and listen to her.

"Ever since we came here you've been... I don't know. Just a bit of a snot. Like you're too good for everyone. Too good for our family. Too good for Tessa and James. And then when you said that thing to Tessa, I just..." She was almost crying. "I don't know. I was really embarrassed. Because you're my twin and I would hate for anyone to not like you. And she was so sweet about it afterwards. She even said that she'd overreacted. But I could see she was really upset." She shook her head. "I just don't understand it. You're not that person. You've always been fun and kind and nice. Where did that come from?"

"I don't know," I mumbled. I shrugged. "I didn't mean..."

But the reality was that I had meant it. And the longer I listened to Charlie, the more ashamed of myself I felt.

"I know you're not supposed to say stuff like this in hospital," she went on. "I just want us to be friends again like we were but I have to tell you the truth."

"I guess I've been jealous of you," I half-whispered. My wrist was going pain-crazy. But maybe it was heart pain and not body pain. "You're so... you know... great."

Charlie looked at me like I was nuts. "Are you for real?" she said. "You're jealous of me? But you're the beautiful one. And you've always had more friends and fitted in better. I look like nothing compared to you."

"But you're so nice. And everyone loves you. And you win at everything," I said. But it felt pathetic.

"I will admit that I can run faster than you," she said. "But it's hardly something that's going to change my life. Or yours. And I'm not really that much nicer than you. I get grumpy too. Maybe the difference is that I go in wanting to like people."

"I guess," I said, and I felt bad. "I'm really sorry."

Charlie smiled and hugged me. "Oops, I'm sorry, I nearly pulled out this thing," and she tugged at the wire in my arm.

"Stop it. You're going to kill me. Do you want to be responsible for the death of your sister?" I said, but I was smiling.

"I don't think I'd do a better job of that than you've already tried," she said. But she was laughing.

Making up with Tessa was easier than I had thought. I was fully prepared to go and explain how wrong I had been and how bad I felt but she waltzed into my hospital room with flowers and chocolates and photographs of the horses the next day as though she didn't even know what Truth or Dare was. I hugged her — genuinely — and then I saw James behind her. For about only the second time ever I saw him give a real, proper, full-sized smile when he saw me. As I've said before, James has an extremely gorgeous smile. And, as I was finding out, it has an extremely good effect on my mood.

I smiled back. And then felt slightly giddy and giggly. Actually, it was nearly as good as the drugs at taking the pain away. *Who needs morphine when the boy you like walks into the room?* I asked myself. Perhaps they needed to give me something to help me breathe though, because as he came closer I found myself running out of oxygen.

"Hey," he said.

"Hey," I answered, which wasn't the world's greatest reply, but I figured he would probably give me some slack, seeing as how I was recovering from major surgery. "Sorry about puking on you. Like, twice." I made a face at him.

"Well, technically once. But there were two lots of puke, that's true," he said. "Still, I guess it can only get better from this point, right?"

"I guess," I said.

"I mean, it can't get much worse..." he began, but I cut him off.

"Stop! You are not allowed to say that!" I said.

"What are you talking about?" he said, smiling at me like I was crazy, and then he looked at me with mushy eyes and I looked back and it was so, so like I was starting to float off on a cloud that I almost couldn't bear it and I had to press on a bruise to bring myself back down to real life. "Owww."

"Are you okay?" He looked so worried about me that I almost laughed out loud.

"Yeah, I'm fine. It just hurts a bit, that's all."

"Well, be careful. Don't move that way," he said, and he turned around to the rest of the people in the room. "Get her another pillow. She needs to rest."

For the next two weeks James was what could only be described as a clucky hen. He came to visit every day from early in the morning until past dinner time or whenever Ness would phone him to tell him he needed to Get Back Here. Now. The Stables Need Mucking Out. Today.

When I finally got discharged and sent home, all we did was talk. We talked about him, about me, about horses, about nothing, about everything. He told me about how he'd liked me the very first time he ever saw me (which I found hard to believe, but I wasn't about to dispute it) and how he'd tried to not show it because he was pretty convinced that I despised him. I tried to tell him that it wasn't true, that I'd also fallen in love with him that day in the paddock, but I was making a new effort to tell the truth about everything and the fib just wouldn't come out of my mouth.

"I think I started to like you, really, that day that I first showed you all I could ride," I said and he laughed. He laughed at almost everything I said now, whether it was funny or not. And he was hanging around the shed endlessly. Tessa and Charlie had to tell him to go away if they wanted to talk with me. I'd let him go, but reluctantly, and I always wanted him to come back. He made me happy. He made me feel like a real person, like someone who was valuable. He made me forget about getting dumped, and how silly and small I felt from all of that. And because he held my hand and told me every day all the things he liked about me (and believe me, there were a lot), I didn't have a single doubt about what I should do when I got this text from Sam a month later.

Hey Coco, wassup? How's the pig shed and the boy next door? Sometimes I miss u. Sammi. PS. We dumped Isabella. Talked too much.

I looked at it, scrunched up my face, and then pressed

the code to block her phone number. I didn't need that kind of aggravation any more. The friends I had now were real friends. People I could trust. People I actually did like.

Yeah, okay, they didn't dress well. But that could be changed—well, at least it could in Tessa's case. I had decided at first that I wasn't going to do any more makeovers because of Charlie telling me I'd been mean, but when Tessa begged me to show her how to do her eye shadow I just couldn't resist. And when she tripped over a pile of clothes that I told her I was about to give to the thrift shop, she pounced on the dreaded floral dress.

"Can I try that on?" she said. "I love it!"

"Too many bad memories for me," I said. "But it actually really suits you." And it was true. She looked amazing in it.

There was no changing James' appearance though. He was still attached to his Cuban heels. "They belonged to my dad. I like wearing them," he protested when I mentioned that perhaps he should update his style. So I learned to look past them, right into his heart.

Finally, I made up with Dad. I was amazed one day when he came up to me asking to talk, and began with an apology. "I'm so sorry, Coco. About all of it. The truth is, I didn't listen to you right from the beginning. But it probably goes back even further. I really didn't even know you back in Sydney. I thought I did, but I'd missed the fact that you had grown up so much."

But by this time I knew he wasn't the only one to blame. "No," I said. "I didn't talk to you. I think we're even."

"But I should have done things differently," he said. "At least talked to you about it over a longer time. It wasn't fair just to pull you out of your life with a click of my fingers and bring you here."

"It didn't feel fair at the time, but Dad, I'm so glad you did. I never want to go back to that school. Or see those people again." I made a face.

"If anyone pushes you in a pool again, you won't be able to stop me," he said. He was laughing, but I could see he was serious. "I'll go in there and tell them where to go."

"Oh, Dad," I cringed. "You can't do that. That's even more embarrassing."

"You think I care about that?" he said. "If people hurt my Coco, I'll come and do something about it."

I looked slightly alarmed. Was he threatening violence? I raised my eyebrows.

"No, I wouldn't hurt anyone," he laughed. "But seriously." His voice got lower. "Make nice friends next year. Go to Pony Camp. Do stuff you're interested in. Find some people who don't do that kind of rubbish."

"I'll try," I said. "I really will."

# CHAPTER 28

The day before my fourteenth birthday, with the cast off my leg and my bruises long gone, we officially moved into our new house.

It wasn't too much hard work. We didn't have much stuff in the shed and a lot of the furniture had already been dragged in once Dad got the walls up and the roof on, but I was a happy girl to pack my suitcase on my bed for the last time and then walk it across the paddock, up a path and through an actual front door which led into an actual hallway and down to an actual bedroom.

We'd all been able to decorate our rooms ourselves, of course. Josh's was bog-standard boy kind of stuff. Plain walls and a checked doona cover. As long as he had enough room for his sound equipment and a cupboard to put his gear in for the second hand motorbike he'd bought with his earnings working for Mum and Ness, he didn't care what else happened.

Charlie's was brighter than before. All the horse pictures were replaced by photos of Fozzles. Plus, she suddenly decided she liked pop art—you know, those old fashioned strip cartoons and super hero kind of images — so she painted cartoon murals all along her wall along with Superman and Wonder Woman figures and was collecting Campbell's tomato soup can labels for a collage.

My room? Well, let's just say I made some changes. I went with Mum one day to the storage container where we had all our old furniture from Sydney, just to remind myself of what was there.

"There's your bed and your dresser, right in the back," said Mum, pointing to a mirror glinting in the light of the torch we'd brought with us.

I clambered over a sofa and a dining table to where I could see it more clearly. The mirrored dressing table I'd begged and scrimped and saved for now looked small and, I hated to say it, a bit tacky.

"It doesn't look right," I said.

"What, is it broken?" came Mum's voice. "I didn't realise. Oh no. The movers must have done it. I knew they weren't being very careful."

"No, it's not broken," I said. "It's just, I don't know. It doesn't look right. It looks wrong. Wrong for me."

"What do you mean?" said Mum.

"I think..." I began. I wasn't sure. "I think I might have outgrown it." I shone my torch along the surface and saw nothing but a blinding glare that hurt my eyes.

"Do you think I could sell it? And maybe get something different? But not something new. I could get like something cheap on eBay and either rub it back or paint it myself. Would you mind?"

"No," said Mum. "That sounds fine. Maybe I can help

you."

"Actually, no," I said. "This is something I think I'd like to do myself."

I could see it in my head. No more purple satin and gold cushions. I wanted everything around me to be hand-made, hand-painted, recycled and re-loved. I wanted it to be beautiful, of course, but an honest kind of beautiful.

And so I got to work. Dad lent me his sander and we made trips back in to Kangaroo Valley Hardware for paint and brushes (chicken feed or fishing tackle anyone?) While I was there I saw the perfect vintage chair for my recycled-and-repainted-from-eBay desk so I bought that too.

No one was allowed in to see anything until I was done, and I wasn't done until our birthday.

Charlie sang *You are my sunshine* to me, of course. In fact, she didn't really stop singing it all day. It got really old after the fifteenth time and now that my plaster was off I could actually chase her to sit on her.

"I'm still faster than you," she said, teasing me. "I just let you catch me."

"You did not. I'm a budding athlete-in-training. I'm going to beat you this year," I said, laughing. "And if you don't stop singing I'm going to beat you up."

"Girls!" said Mum. "Coco, get off her. Come and get your presents."

Two enormous boxes, identically wrapped and both with big blue bows, sat on the floor.

"Oh yeah!" said Charlie. "Let's do this."

We read the tags to find out who's was whose, then

sat in front of them, and with perfect coordination, pulled the bows and ripped the paper to get inside at the same time.

"It doesn't matter," said Josh, laughing at us. "You know it's not going to be the same thing anyway. You could, like, be individuals if you wanted."

"Josh!" said Dad. "Let them do it the way they like."

"Anyway," said Mum. "Maybe you're wrong..."

Josh was wrong. Our presents were identical. I had assumed that Mum had just found two big boxes to fill up with different things, but not this year.

We pulled open the boxes, jamming our fingers into tape and cardboard and almost forgetting to stay coordinated in our haste to find out what was inside. I got to mine first.

"Oh Mum! Wow!" I shouted. Yes, I know. Shouting about birthday presents is kind of juvenile but some things deserve to be shouted about, and a brand new, gleaming, black leather saddle is one of them.

"Me too!" yelled Charlie. (See? We're more alike than we think.) "A saddle!"

"This is the coolest thing ever," I said. "And look, a matching bridle and reins." I pulled them out and dangled them in front of Charlie's face. "It's all sooo gorgeous."

Mum was smiling and Dad looked pleased.

"We thought you needed a saddle, Charlie, because you've been using Tessa's old one and Coco, I never want to hear about you going bareback riding again!"

"Oh, this is so great," I said. "Look how beautiful it is. Hopefully it'll fit Cupcake."

"Well, that's another thing," said Mum. She looked at Dad. They both looked out the shed door. "Oh, here they come."

"What?" said Charlie. "What's out there?"

I ran to the door and nearly fell over. Walking up the paddock were Tessa, James and Ness, and behind them were two horses.

One of which was Cupcake.

"Are we going for a ride?" I said. "Testing out the new saddles?"

"More like testing out your new horses, really," said Mum.

"What?" I yelled. (Again with the yelling.) "Are you kidding? Cupcake is my horse now? My very own?"

"Well, I didn't think Charlie would want her," Mum said smiling.

"You. Are. Kidding. Me." I whooped, jumping around the floor. "This is unbelievable. I have a horse!"

I stopped to look at Charlie but she was already halfway down the paddock with her arms around Fozzles' neck. Tessa was smiling and Ness was laughing and James was standing back, looking at everything like he always does, but I like that about him. He's thoughtful and he doesn't need to be in the spotlight and he says what he thinks and it's usually right. But then he looked up at me and he smiled, a big wide smile, and I smiled back and I ran down to see him and I wanted to hug him and even kiss him but his mum and Tessa were right there and I knew Josh would never let me live it down if I did anything, so instead I shyly took Cupcake's lead rope from him, but he didn't let go, and the two of us walked Cupcake up to the shed together.

"Happy birthday," he said.

"Thanks," I said.

"It's a nice day for it," he said.

"Yes," I said, looking around. The sun was playing in a velvet blue sky with white fluffy clouds and air that smelt real and fresh, and rays of light were bouncing on grass so green that it looked like it came straight out of a child's paint set. "It really, really is."

Mum's idea was to have our birthday dinner in the new house but I asked if we could have it outside instead, picnic style. The evening was perfect and I was starting to find that I needed to be outside more and more or I felt like I'd been missing out.

"Plus, this way the horses can join in," I said. "Cupcake is a birthday horse now. She needs to be there."

Mum raised her eyebrows. "I am not feeding a horse Thai green chicken curry and tiramisu cake," she said. "Cupcake can watch from the other side of the fence." She relented when she saw my pretend sad face. "Okay, I'll let you give her a carrot. But she's not getting near the food."

We didn't have all our things unpacked yet so Mum had bought temporary red plastic plates for Charlie and me.

"It's our celebration thing," Charlie explained to Tessa who looked confused. "The birthday person always gets the red plate."

"You guys have the most amazing view," said Ness, sitting herself down on the picnic rug and stretching her arms in front of her. "You've built the house in the perfect spot. Those morning sunrises are going to be fantastic."

Dad looked modest. "Well, it'll be good when we get the verandas built. It's still not finished..."

"But it's great, sweetheart," said Mum. "You know it is."

"Yeah, and I think we should build some stables next," said Charlie.

"And what about a course for motor bikes too, and maybe even some jumps?" said Josh. He looked at James, whose face lit up.

"No!" said Mum and Dad and Ness, together. Josh and James looked back, surprised.

"We've already had one accident," said Dad. "One broken leg is enough. Definitely no bike jumps. Two wheels on the ground at all times." He raised his eyes at Josh who shrugged and rolled his eyes.

"I don't need the face," said Dad. "Deal with it. Anyway, it's cake time."

Mum brought out the tiramisu decorated with 28 lighted candles and put it down carefully in front of Charlie and me. The breeze made the flames dance.

"Happy birthday, girls," she said, laughing and trying to guard the fire with her hands. "We hope you have a great year."

We blew out the candles together and then picked up a knife each, ready to cut it when Dad said something.

"Before you do that, I have an announcement to make."

My heart skipped a beat and my hand froze up. Was Dad for real? Didn't he know I wanted to actually eat my birthday cake this year? Surely he couldn't have another bombshell to drop on us. I hardly wanted to look at him just in case he wasn't joking.

"This time last year we started our big move. Now we've got a new house, new friends, new interests and new possibilities. You guys have all been great and it's been so fun to do this with you, but..." and here he stopped.

I hadn't breathed yet and I was about to topple over so I quickly gulped some air and went back to my frozen state.

"... but I'm guessing you might like to get back to normal a bit now," he said.

"What do you mean?" said Josh.

"Aren't we normal?" said Charlie, looking pretend-offended. "I'm normal, right?"

"You don't mean go back to Sydney do you?" I said, horrified. "I can't do that!"

"Yes, Charlie, you're normal. And no, Coco, I'm not talking about going back to Sydney. I'm talking about going back to school. I'm sure you're sick of being at home by now, and the house is built, so what do you think?"

I was so relieved that I dropped the knife right into the tiramisu. Amazingly, it fell straight, made a perfect cut and stopped just before it hit the cake board.

"Wow, look at that," said Tessa. "That's cool."

"I think that means yes," I said. "School sounds excellent."

Tessa clapped her hands. "Yay! You can come with us."

I smiled at her and then looked back down at my

knife.

"You can make a wish," said James. "It didn't touch the plate."

"Yeah, I can," I said. But instead of closing my eyes to wish I opened them up wide and looked around at the house and the paddocks, at Cupcake hanging her head over the fence wanting to come up, and at the sky and the clouds turning all orange-pink.

*I wish for beauty just like this,* I said to myself. *I wish for good friends at school. And I wish for James to kiss me.*

Yes, I know. It was more than one wish. But I think the wish fairies, wherever they live, will be able to cope. And anyway, I'm not so sure that wishes are really very reliable. I think it's more about what you make of what you've got. I mean, I was hoping for popularity last year and I got a whole lot of muddy puddles instead. But when it all got sorted out, it turned out it was better to get covered in mud than to be part of a group that did nothing but throw mud at other people.

(By the way, at least one of my wishes came true later that evening. You'll have to guess which one, of course. And later, another of the wishes came true as well. But all of that is for a whole other story.)

THE END

# ACKNOWLEDGEMENTS

Thanks to the Banks family for the inspiration for the story, especially to the real Coco, who is nothing like the book Coco and certainly hasn't suffered through nearly as many embarrassing, muddy or vomit-filled situations. She's also incredibly generous and not selfish at all and has excellent taste in footwear (although she doesn't wear ballet flats much). And I'm sure she's never had such big fights with her sister, the real Charlie, who is also lovely, funny and very talented.

Thanks to the real Ness for the horse advice. I learned a lot about round yards and body language and horse whispering. I also will probably never ever use the word 'whinny' again. (Apparently horses are much quieter animals than I thought.)

Thanks to the kind test readers who gave me useful feedback: Shelley A, Jessy L, Jenny S, Joana H (who got into trouble with her mum because she was reading it when she was supposed to be going to sleep... sorry Mum!), Rebecca A, Linda T, Myra, Heaven A, Gillian E,

Ashton S, Nicole P, Heather Y, Lynne S who suggested some first chapter revisions, and others.

Thanks always to my husband who is always supportive and fixes my computer problems, and to our local preschool staff who entertain and educate my own little Coco while I'm writing.

This story is fictional. I made up everything Coco did, said and thought. But it is based on real life circumstances, people and places. Yes, Budgong and Kangaroo Valley really exist. You can get a coffee at Charlie's cafe, you can check out rocking horses at the Wood Shop and you can buy fishing tackle and a whole lot of other stuff at the hardware place.

You can also go for a horse ride through the amazing Aussie bush (and maybe even meet some familiar characters) if you book at www.kangaroovalleyhorses.com.au.

# ABOUT THE AUTHOR

Cecily Anne Paterson has given up sugar in pursuit of a more healthy lifestyle more times than she can count. She prefers dogs over cats, acoustic guitar over electric and tea over coffee. She'd be very happy to never have to cook again in her life, although it's not looking likely that that particular miracle will ever occur. She lives with her husband, four children and two dogs in small town New South Wales, Australia. Her literary aim is to write two books a year for the next ten years.

You can follow Cecily Anne Paterson on Facebook, Pinterest or Twitter and on her website at www.cecilypaterson.com

# Also by Cecily Anne Paterson

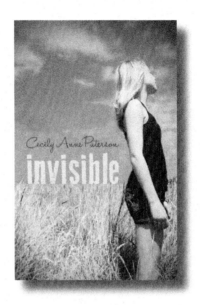

## Invisible

The first story in the notable *Invisible* series.

A semi-finalist in the Amazon Breakthrough Novel Award 2014.

"Lovely... sensitive, hopeful, empowering"

~ Cathy Cassidy

"Invisible is... an exquisitely written story... a stunning account of the reinvention of a compelling and sympathetic character."

~Publisher's Weekly

www.cecilypaterson.com

## Invincible

In book two of the popular *Invisible* series, 13 year old Jazmine isn't the girl that nobody notices any more. But it's still complicated. For starters, she can't sleep at night. And then there's Liam. He's totally gorgeous; everyone agrees with that. So why does Jaz feel so bad and so guilty when she's around him?
When everything seems to be falling to pieces around her, will she be courageous enough to face up to her biggest fears?

www.cecilypaterson.com

# COMING SOON
*from Cecily Anne Paterson*

## Smart Girls Don't Wear Mascara

Abby Smart has her life sorted out. She's top of the class,
she has two awesome best friends, and she's going to be a singer.
But when new girl Stella appears on the scene, everything seems
to fall apart. Why can't everyone else see what Abby sees in Stella?
And why is Stella ruining her life?

*The first book in the new Kangaroo Valley School series*

CPSIA information can be obtained
at www.ICGtesting.com
Printed in the USA
LVOW13s0121020217
522956LV00034B/907/P